Val Daniels says she'll try anything once, from waitress to market researcher, from library aide to consensus coordinator. But her real love has always been writing. Val lives with her husband, two children and a "Murphy dog" in Kansas.

Val Daniels' previous book, *Forever Isn't Long Enough*, was highly praised and won the 1996 *Write Touch: Readers' Award* organized by the Wisconsin Romance Writers of America.

"A touching love story brimming with witty dialogue and characters that leap off the page and into our hearts."

—*Romantic Times*

"Delightfully romantic story. The characters are warm and captivating... I loved it!"

—*Rendezvous*

Dear Reader,

Hmm? A bakery and Valentine's Day? What do the two have to do with each other? For me, baking has been irrevocably entwined with Valentine's Day since the first time I was old enough to have a sweetheart. The fad at the time was baking a "sweetheart" cake.

I remember going to the store with my best friend to find heart-shaped pans. We chose a Red Devil's Food Cake recipe and added lots of red food coloring. And though the "Valentine" I baked it for is a rare glimmer in my thoughts, I have wonderful memories of spending an entire day fussing over and decorating that bright red cake. (Surely, the cake turned out well or I'd remember, don't you think?)

Oddly, most of my "special" Valentine memories are not of what I received, but of things that brought me joy in giving. Things like homemade, lace-doily valentines. Things I made with my hands.

So from my hands—and my heart—this is my Valentine to you. I hope you love the special, belated Valentine gift Brad makes for Autumn as much as I loved "baking" it up for you.

Wishing you love and joy,

Sweet Valentine
Val Daniels

Harlequin Books

TORONTO • NEW YORK • LONDON
AMSTERDAM • PARIS • SYDNEY • HAMBURG
STOCKHOLM • ATHENS • TOKYO • MILAN
MADRID • WARSAW • BUDAPEST • AUCKLAND

For Ned and Reba Harmon.
Thanks, Mom and Dad,
for your guidance, love, encouragement—
and for always believing I could do better.

ISBN 0-373-03446-6

SWEET VALENTINE

First North American Publication 1997.

CHAPTER ONE

THE BELL OVER THE DOOR clanged and Autumn Sanderford shook herself from her pensive mood and pasted on her most gracious smile. Setting aside the growing stack of papers she'd been gathering from the files, she straightened her shoulders and rose from the small stool behind the cash register. As her eyes met the incoming customer's, she wished she hadn't sent Elaine home. No one should have to greet the man she saw coming toward the counter looking the way she knew she looked.

Darn it! He was to-die-for, drop-dead perfect and she was certain she looked like something the cat wouldn't drag in.

Rising at four-thirty every morning for the past six months was taking its toll and she'd noticed that the dark circles under her eyes were becoming more and more prominent. The horrible hair-net thing the health department required food service people to wear was not at all becoming though it did eliminate the daily worry about what to do with her thick, wavy, unmanageable hair. By this time of day, a couple of those strands had escaped. If she didn't have at least one smudge of flour on her face, it was not a normal day. And lately, getting out of bed had become so difficult she'd quit bothering with makeup.

The man's blue-green eyes met and dazzled her from across the top of the two-foot pastry case.

"May I help you?" She gave in to the urge to check her face for flour, then brushed at the powdery substance she found on her cheek.

His grin widened as his eyes followed the gesture. "You missed a spot," he said, tapping his own temple.

Her hand moved to the approximate spot on her own forehead and she scrubbed at it lightly. She knew she missed it again when his wonderfully white smile spread an extra sparkle to the beautifully bright eyes. "Here, would you like me—"

"Never mind." She broke in as he reached toward her across the case. "I'm sure I'll eventually get used to wearing flour instead of makeup."

His smile tilted.

"Now, what can I do for you?"

"I hear you make very impressive cookie bouquets?"

She nodded, certain her grin had widened to match his. *That* was why she was here. Not the doughnuts and baked goods she sold one at a time to people on their coffee breaks.

"Do you have a brochure or somethi—"

"Let me get my book." She swiveled to retrieve the white three-ring binder she and the photographer had so carefully put together months and months ago. Too few customers had looked at it and the book had gradually made its way to the top corner of her desk, out of the way of fingers sticky from sticky buns, doughnut glaze and apple fritter crumbs.

It was filled with photos of the kind of bouquets she could do. Get Well ones, with teddy bear cookies dressed like doctors and nurses. Bouquets for every holiday, from Halloween to the Fourth of July and everything in between.

Instead of handing it across to him, she walked around the end of the counter and placed it on one of the small side tables, inviting him to sit down. "Could I get you a cup of coffee while you look?"

One of his eyebrows raised slightly.

What? What had she done wrong, she wanted to ask. His expressive face cleared and she suspected her imagination was working overtime.

"I'd love a cup," he accepted her invitation, pulling out the chair beside the table.

She went to the other side of the room to the small coffee bar. Of course, he'd been a little surprised at her offer of coffee. He couldn't have missed the large Serve Yourself sign over the coffee machine. Maybe she *was* acting a little overeager. She slowed her footsteps and forced herself not to rush back to him.

"If I can get you anything else...?" Autumn set the hot paper cup beside the hand he'd rested on the table.

"Do you have questions? Something specific in mind? The prices listed are for six cookies, but I can easily do eight or four. Whatever you want. And I can design almost any kind of cookie you would want in your..." Her words died away as he quirked that eyebrow again "...bouquet," she finished. This time, there was no denying the raised eyebrow. And could she blame him? She had practically pounced on him. "Just let me know if you...if I can answer any question. Any question at all." She cleared her throat.

Seconds later, he waved toward the chair on the opposite side of the table. "Would you care to join me?"

Her face grew hot when she realized she was fidgeting and hovering as he turned the pages. "Just wanted to be helpful. I have—'' she flung a gesture toward some vague spot behind the counter ''—work to do.''

He coolly surveyed the empty bakery then looked up at her again. She glanced down at her clasped hands and saw white knuckles. Commanding herself to ease her grip, she squared her shoulders and lifted her head. ''This time of day is always slow, right before the coffee crowd hits. I generally try to get some of my extra work done now.''

Sure, his expression seemed to say. ''I won't keep you then.'' He waited for her to go away.

Autumn took two steps backward then spun and scurried toward the safety of the kitchen. She felt his eyes on her every inch of the way.

Once behind the swinging doors, she leaned against the wall and put the back of her hands to her heated cheeks.

He was interested in her cookie bouquets, for heaven's sake. Why was she acting as if her whole life depended on him ordering one?

Maybe because it did, she admitted to herself. Maybe because if she didn't do something soon, she was going to lose this business and every cent of her investment. Besides her dream dying this slow, painful and very unexciting death, she was going to have to go to her father and admit he had been right. Or borrow money. He *had* offered.

Both choices made her sick with frustration. There had to be—

Something clicked in her mind. She went to the bulletin board where she'd stuck the business card Jen had given her last week. Barnett Marketing. It was a long shot. She couldn't afford it. *But it can't hurt to check it out,* her best friend's words echoed in that same logical tone she'd used as long as Autumn had known her.

And it was now or never. She'd call and make an appointment as soon as the man in the other room left.

Why hadn't she made one of her sample bouquets today? The brightly decorated cookies on sticks, looking like huge lollipops until she put them in the woven wicker flower baskets and surrounded them with colorful tissue paper and a huge bow, didn't look nearly as impressive in pictures as they did for real. She battled the urge to peek out and see what he was doing.

There wasn't a thing to do in here. The white glossy painted surfaces around her were spotless. The stainless-steel industrial-size appliances gleamed under the bright, long tubes of fluorescent light.

Her eyes went to the clock on the wall. The minute hand crept ever closer to ten o'clock and she prayed the man would order something and leave soon. Or maybe there would be a real miracle. Maybe one or two of the coffee "crowd" she'd referred to a minute ago would find her shop today.

As if in answer to her prayer, the bell over the door sounded again. This time, she didn't have to plaster on the smile. It bloomed naturally. As soon as she helped this customer, she'd casually ask Mr. Cookie Bouquet if he'd found an appropriate design for whatever occasion he wanted one for.

The grin on her face froze into a grimace as she pushed through the door. The man who had been looking at her book was on the opposite side of the glass display windows, walking toward a brand-new pewter-colored car.

And once again, the bakery was empty.

The January wind rippled the man's dark hair and he shrugged up the collar of his coat. She ducked down behind the counter as he started to fold his long frame into the sports car. If he happened to glance back, she didn't want him to catch her gazing at him forlornly.

Brad Barnett—Marketing Consultant

Autumn thumbed the side of the business card. She double-checked the number on the front of the house against the address on the rich cardstock. Jennifer had said Brad Barnett's ideas had taken her husband's business from barely paying the bills to a monthly profit of nearly five figures in two short months. The way Jen talked, his card should say Miracle Worker.

But would a successful marketing consultant work out of his home?

Obviously he would, Autumn decided as she slowly climbed out of her car and hesitated, looking around to see if there was another entrance besides the front door. One that said: Entrance or something to indicate that this was also a business.

She didn't see a thing.

Pulling her gloves and rearranging her scarf more securely to keep out the icy breeze, she made her way to the front of the magnificent house and rang the bell.

The door opened almost instantly.

A beautiful woman, whose middle-age was betrayed only by the smile lines around her eyes, greeted her warmly. "Do come in, Miss Sanderford. We've been expecting you. And right on time, too."

Keeping up a steady stream of chatter, she closed out the frigid air and took Autumn's coat. The woman draped it over her arm, slipped into a room off the foyer and indicated that Autumn should follow.

With a wave of her hand, she steered Autumn to a chair beside a softly glowing fireplace. "Mr. Barnett will be with you in just a minute. He went to— Oh, there you are Brad. This is Miss Sanderford."

Only half-settled in the comfortable chair, Autumn redirected her energy to getting back up again. As she smoothed the long camel colored skirt she'd paired with a sweater, she turned to greet the man. Her hand froze somewhere between her side and the full extension she planned to offer him.

"Ah. The cookie bouquet lady." His smooth as cream voice flowed over her.

His hand closed the gap between her partially extended one and his grip clasped her firmly. "What perfect timing," he said. "We've been putting together an order for you. Betty, you can give it directly to Miss Sanderford when she leaves. She's the owner of Sweet Sensations." He explained to Betty then looked to Autumn for confirmation.

The tingling sensations charging from his hand into hers, and running up her arm had nothing to do with cookie bouquets or anything sweet. Autumn managed to nod mutely as he let go of her hand.

"I'm glad you're here." He steered her back toward her chair and dismissed Betty all at one time. "When I was in your shop yesterday, I thought it was a real shame that you had such an interesting product and were doing such a dismal job of marketing it," he said bluntly, easing his long frame onto the corner of his huge desk.

Autumn felt her back stiffen and her face grow hot.

"I'm glad you're savvy enough to realize you need help."

Stab with one hand, stroke with the other. The man was as smoothly deceptive as a gnarled hand inside a silk glove. He smiled lazily, giving her a chance to catch her breath.

"When I called for the appointment, I thought you'd be older." Dammit! She finally had a chance to say something and she managed to say something totally inane.

"And as charming as I thought you were with flour on your face, you're just as beautiful without it."

She opened and shut her mouth several times without uttering a word.

He seemed satisfied that he'd rendered her speechless. "If my age bothers you because you're afraid I lack experience let me assure you that I don't. I know marketing backward, forward and upsidedown." He said it lightly. "And if you'd like references..." He made the statement a question and let it drift.

"No. I have a reference. I mean, a friend told me about you. That wasn't what I meant. I was just surprised, that's all. Especially when you...you..." she said.

"Dress in jeans?"

She wished he wouldn't have mentioned the jeans. She'd been trying to avoid looking at the way they hugged his muscular thighs, trying not to notice how his sweater draped down and sort of emphasized...other parts of his anatomy. She swallowed hard and looked back up at him—

—and wished there was a hole in the floor she could fall through. The knowing glimmer in his eyes said he could guess exactly what she was thinking. Darn it, the man knew how attractive he was and was enjoying every minute of her discomfort.

"I don't have any trouble with the way you dress," she said primly. "But when I saw your office was in your house, I just thought you must be retired or—"

"I am retired." He crossed his arms over his chest and managed to look even mo_e smug. "That should tell you how good I am at what I do. Which is why you need me," he added arrogantly. "And I do have ideas for getting your cookie bouquet business off the ground. Isn't that why you made the appointment to see me?"

What could she say? She nodded and somehow dragged her eyes from his brilliant ones. Maybe if she didn't look at him, she would be able to pretend he was the kind, grandfatherly type she'd expected.

"I've brought—" she leaned over and opened the portfolio case she'd set beside her chair "—my notebook to give you some idea of—"

"I saw that yesterday. Remember?"

She let her arm sag and the heavy book fell back into the bag with a thud.

Grinning, he moved to the opposite side of his desk and pulled a notepad toward him as he sat down. "Let me ask you a few questions about your business and the results you want. We'll make more progress."

Ninety minutes later, Mr. Brad Barnett, marketing consultant extraordinaire, leaned against the high back of his leather chair and sighed. Dazed and drained from the enormous amount of information he'd drawn from her in that short period of time, Autumn let herself relax. She could understand why he was so cocky. His questions had made her re-examine her expectations and what she really wanted from her business. She'd had to put into words concepts she'd only held in her head the two years before she'd started and the seven months since she'd actually been working in her little venture. And his questions had already generated an idea or two about things she, herself, could do. "All right. I'll admit it. You're good," she conceded with a smile.

He lifted his chin a smidge. "And how would you know whether I'm good or not?"

She was suddenly speechless again, groping for words.

His soft chuckle relaxed her again. "Wait until you see me do my thing before you decide I'm good," he drawled, his eyelids slowly dropping to half-mast. They mesmerized her and gave his words a very different meaning in her mind. And she had the feeling that he would be very good at that, too.

She straightened her back and crossed her legs at the knees. "You're right. I should wait for results before judging." She was reading all sorts of things into his words that probably weren't there.

But something in the predatory way he moved as he came around the edge of the desk toward her made her feel as jumpy as a hunted cat. He *was* the best looking man she'd seen in a lifetime. She cleared her throat. "I guess I should have said you *seem* to be a master at what you do," she added, then realized she still hadn't mentioned business. "At marketing," she amended.

The crinkles at the corner of his eyes held amusement as he resettled sideways on the edge of his desk, dangling one long leg in front of her as he propped himself up with the other. "Are you a master at what you do? At making cookie bouquets," he added, mocking her.

Her heart settled a beat or two, to a dull thud. "I'm not getting much of a chance."

"That's why you're here." His wry smile seemed to indicate that he was willing to go back to business if she wasn't interested in responding to his subtle overtures.

She nodded. "Oh. That reminds me." She reached into her heavy sachel and pulled out a thin box. "I thought you should have an opportunity to sample the product and see exactly what I do if you are going to help me market it." She frowned as she lifted the lid. "I hope I didn't break them when I dropped the book."

"The crumbs should taste as good as the whole," he offered as she drew the tissue away from the cookies. "Of course I don't have that philosophy about everything," he added. "I've never been especially happy about accepting crumbs."

For a second, there was a tense charge in the air as his eyes reprimanded her for ignoring his earlier come-ons. Then Autumn laughed. "I don't imagine you are." She held up a cookie she'd decorated like a neon sign advertising "Barnett Marketing."

"So what do you think? I couldn't think of a symbol for a marketing firm. That particular cookie is low-cal, fat-free. And this one—" She gently turned

the shape she'd worked the hardest on so he could
see it in the box.

"This one, I'm really proud of." In this cookie,
she'd managed to catch the essence of a newspaper,
spread to show the headline on the front page. It had
taken her at least a dozen disasters to get the look she
wanted. The headline said Read All About It.

"You managed to make it look like actual news-
print." His voice held the right touch of admiration.

"It took a lot of time and experimentation. I ended
up—"

His finger against her lips stopped her. "I don't
need the details. I'm not planning on going into the
business."

She went still, then smiled as he lowered his finger.

"And in this instance, I would think the proof is
in the pudding... or the cookie as the case might be."
He bit into the neon sign. "I'd say you've mastered
low-cal, no fat," he added quickly.

"Thank you." She felt a flush appearing. "The rest
are a mixture of the regular sugar cookies—I make
them pretty well if I do say so myself—and the lemon-
flavored, low-cal ones. I also do an artificially
sweetened recipe for diabetics, but I didn't bring a
sample of that." She rearranged them in the box. "Do
you think your secretary might want one? Betty, didn't
you say? The rest are just flowers. That's the way I
fill out each bouquet. And I think they do look attractive. I'll leave you with—"

"Has anyone ever told you you babble when you're
nervous?"

She looked up at him, startled. A cookie crumb
decorated the edge of his mouth and she revised his

earlier remark. She thought she might be perfectly happy to accept his crumbs.

Nibbling at her own lip self-consciously, Autumn looked away quickly when his tongue dipped out to retrieve the tiny bit of cookie.

She rose and set the box on the edge of his desk, knowing she was way past due to leave. For her own sake. Before she did something really stupid.

Providentially, Betty poked her head back in the door. "You have a call," she told Brad after she apologized for interrupting. "Line two. I think it's important."

Autumn hadn't heard the phone ring. His home-based office must be equipped with fairly sophisticated technology.

He picked up the phone and Autumn, with Betty's assistance, escaped.

"I'll be in touch soon," he mouthed as she raised her hand in a goodbye.

"Thank you," she mouthed back.

Within minutes, she was in the eight-year-old economy car her father had given her as a high school graduation present, backing out of his driveway. Before she was out of his neighborhood, she had a mile-long mental list of questions she hadn't asked and things she hadn't made clear.

That's what happens when your mind isn't on where it's supposed to be, she could almost hear her father's voice, thick with censure. And he'd be right this time. Her mind hadn't been focused on business, not totally anyway.

The minute she got home, she'd make a list to make sure he didn't sidetrack her and then call him. Maybe not having him in the same room, looking at her the way a mountain climber might look at a mountain he wanted to conquer, she wouldn't be so distracted. She should discuss her limited budget—or the lack of one. How could you have a budget if you didn't have money to spend on the items budgeted? she wondered.

And how could she have forgotten to ask Brad how he'd happened on her shop yesterday? She slammed her palm against the steering wheel.

As if in response to her mistreatment, the little car suddenly died. No sputter, no jolt, no radio. Everything just went dead.

"Oh, please don't do this to me," she moaned. Without the benefit of power steering, she had to tug the wheel hard to negotiate to the side of the street. She coasted to a stop about two feet from the curb, blocking the mailbox, half blocking the driveway to one of the lavish homes.

She leaned her head against the steering wheel and prayerfully begged the car to forgive her for her impulsive misbehavior. But when she turned the key in the ignition, nothing happened.

She leaned back against the seat, puffed up at the soft bangs against her forehead and looked around. Unlike the newer homes they were building like crazy on Brad's block, the house she was in front of had a large yard and was set back from the road a bit. It reminded her of the house she'd grown up in in a similar neighborhood across town. Very little crime, neighbors who watched the neighborhood—and each other—like hawks. Someone was probably calling the police even now, reporting suspicious activity.

The January day was crisp, but the late-afternoon sun was bright. It felt warm on her face as she got out and trudged across the wide expanse of cushiony brown lawn. No one answered when she pressed the doorbell.

She could probably set off an alarm just by going over and touching one of the windows. *That* would bring help. She suddenly realized that she didn't *want* help.

She wanted to go back to Brad's.

She decided she'd better do it soon, before help of some sort or another arrived. Before she didn't have an excuse.

Brad answered the door himself this time. Autumn gave him a bright smile as he looked around her toward the driveway.

"I had car trouble," she told him quickly. "Could I use your phone?"

"Where's your car?" He frowned and opened the door wider for her.

"A couple of blocks from here," she explained, stepping inside.

"Anything I can do?" He rocked forward on the Spanish tiled floor of the foyer as if he was ready to grab his coat and a wrench or something and go forth to be a hero.

"I have AAA. Just let me call them."

"What seemed to be the problem?"

Why did men always insist on asking what was wrong with a car? She was a mechanically impaired female, for heaven's sake. If she knew what was wrong, she probably wouldn't need him or his phone. "I have no idea what's wrong," she said. "It just died."

He looked almost disappointed as he lead her back into his office and reached across his desk for the cordless telephone receiver.

"Push the On button," he directed as she sat down in the seat where she'd sat earlier and looked through her wallet for her AAA card.

He perched himself on the corner of his desk again and listened intently as she gave the necessary information to the woman who answered the call.

"Thanks," she said a few minutes later as she handed the phone back to him. "It'll be forty-five minutes to an hour." She rose hesitantly.

"You may as well wait here."

"I don't want to keep you from anything..."

"When you rang the doorbell, I was in the kitchen, pouring myself some soda. Could I get you something?"

She didn't realize how thirsty she was until he offered it. She sank back into her seat. "That would be wonderful."

She knew she'd sounded stilted and formal when he grinned and said, "I wasn't offering to wait on you. Come on in the kitchen. We'll be more comfortable."

The room he took her to was more than a kitchen. One end of it fit the description by holding cabinets, countertops and appliances, but the rest of the room was obviously where he spent his leisure time.

A huge TV filled one corner. A chair sat by another fireplace, this one unlit. The soft leather sofa was in direct line with the TV. It seemed to still hold his form. She could almost picture him, lying there, watching TV. Another chair, complete with a matching footstool strewn with the morning paper, occupied a niche beside an end table. Windows stretched across the entire back wall.

She wanted this room. Without putting forth a bit of energy, she could see herself puttering around the kitchen, with him stretched out on—

"Here, let me take your coat." His hands settled on her shoulders, sending warmth down her arms. She shrugged out of the heavy trench coat and stepped quickly away from him. He draped it across the back of the overstuffed couch.

He took the lead again, crossing and pulling out a high stool beside the tiled countertop separating the country-style kitchen from the rest of the room.

On the opposite side of the counter, a half-full glass of ice sat beside a large bottle of soda, a testament that he'd been doing exactly what he said when she interrupted him. He opened the cabinet behind him and reached for a glass as she spied the coffeemaker sitting beside the stove.

"Could I have a cup of coffee instead?" she asked.

His hand stopped in midair, changed directions and withdrew one of the mugs from the shelf beside the glasses. He touched the half-empty coffeepot. "It's lukewarm. Betty probably shut it off at least an hour ago."

"We could warm it in the microwave."

His grin tilted to one side as he poured coffee into the mug and pushed a couple of buttons on the microwave set into the wall of cabinets. As he returned to the bottle of soda and started filling his glass, he gazed at her. "I do like people who know what they want."

His low voice flowed over her like whiskey over ice, crackling, smoothing edges, splintering her concentration. One of his eyelids drooped lazily, half wink, half blink.

Darn it, the man was dangerous. As dangerous as playing with fire. And if *she* was pouring something without watching what she was doing, she'd have a mess everywhere.

As if reading her thoughts, he looked down to check his progress then set the bottle down and recapped it.

She glanced at the clock on the wall behind him. Only five minutes had passed since she'd finished her call.

"We have about half an hour," he said, noting the direction of her gaze. "Perfect. I like getting to know my clients personally. Makes it easier to do a good job."

The "personally" made her fidgety. "I think we should discuss how we'll—"

"Business hours are over," he interrupted.

"After I left, I thought of a million things I should have told or asked you."

One eyebrow quirked upward, one lowered.

"We didn't talk about your fees. As I told your secretary when I made the appointment, I don't know if I can afford you."

"You can't afford *not* to have me." A long, steady look dared her to disagree. Then he turned to retrieve her mug from the microwave. "It'll all be included in the proposal I'll bring you." He set the coffee in front of her. "Next week," he added as she opened her mouth to ask another question. He took a drink from his glass and set it aside, dispensing with it as determinedly as he had dispensed with office hours. "Now, that should take care of any loose ends as far as business is concerned. Let's talk about . . . you."

CHAPTER TWO

AUTUMN SQUIRMED uncomfortably.

He leaned across the counter, propping himself on his elbows. His face was less than a foot from hers.

She focused her attention on the hands she'd clasped around her mug. "What do you want to know?"

"Oh...vital statistics, maybe." He shrugged. "Are you married? Have you ever been?"

His question took her by such surprise that for a second, she just stared at him. Then she burst into laughter. She couldn't believe what this handsome, seemingly perfect, thirty-four or -five year old male had just said.

His scowl deepened.

"You said the *m* word," she reminded him. "Marriage," she added when he continued to frown.

He smiled slyly. "Well, at least I don't have to ask my next question. You obviously aren't seriously involved with anyone or you wouldn't be so shocked that someone mentioned the word."

She leaned back further in her seat, putting a little more distance between them. The man was much too intense, even when he was being foolish. And those eyes.

"It's the next logical question," he explained. "When you meet someone, what are the questions you ask first? Occupation? I know that. Where you live? I know that. Where you grew up. You told me you were born and raised in Johnson County when I asked you why you chose the location you did for your business. I know your eyes are hazel and that they sparkle when you're amused. I know your hair is light brown with a touch of..." He fingered a strand of her hair, which had escaped from the big bow holding it halfway neatly at the back of her neck, examining it in the fading light of day "...champagne? Is that a hair color?" He smoothed the strand back against her shoulder then stood up straight. He narrowed his eyes and looked what he could see of her up and down. "I'd guess you're five foot six or seven and weigh maybe..."

"Enough!" Autumn held up her hand. "If you have a guess, don't tell me. I don't want to know." With him a safe distance away, Autumn could suddenly breath again.

His eyes said he thought her weight was just about right as he shrugged. "So what is one of the next logical questions in the 'getting-to-know-you' game? Marital status. Even though I think I have it figured out, I thought it would be polite to ask."

She laughed again and shook her head. Only someone as arrogant and self-assured as Brad Barnett could say "Are you married? Have you ever been?" all in the same breath and call it polite conversation. "How about you? Are you—"

"Oh? You want to know my height and weight?" He reached for his back pocket as if to pull out his wallet and his driver's license as proof.

She shook her head. "That's okay. You can just tell me. I'll take your word for it."

"Six-two. One hundred eighty-six pounds."

"And the other? Are you—or have you ever been—married?" she asked sweetly, expecting him to twitch nervously.

"Nope," he answered nonchalantly. "But I'm looking." In half a second, he'd turned the tables neatly back on her and left her groping for something to say again.

Her mind raced. He seemed deadly serious. The whole conversation was making her crazy. With most guys, it was wise to avoid the subject like the plague. Not that she minded their attitude as much as most of her friends did; she'd always found the whole idea mystical, something to think about at some later date. Brad made her feel as intimidated as she suspected most males did when the issue came up.

"Th . . . that's nice." She cleared her throat. "What about the rest? The 'getting-to-know-you' game has been pretty one-sided so far. I know your occupation but I have no idea where you're from." She sighed as quietly as she could, relieved that she'd changed the subject without giving in to her overwhelming, desperate, nervous urge to start babbling.

His lip twitched but the gleam in his eye was admiring. She had the feeling he could read every thought. She wondered where he had learned that trick. Was mind reading something he'd taken in college? Could she sign—

She realized she was babbling inwardly now and in danger of missing his answer.

"—in Chicago. South side. Not exactly the picture-perfect childhood. I was the bad boy your mother probably warned you about when you left home."

Autumn didn't doubt it for an instant. "But you aren't now?"

He shook his head. "Those years are long behind me."

"So how did you wind up in Kansas City?"

"Long story," he warned.

She glanced at her watch. "I have a while."

He told her about getting a football scholarship to a college in Ohio, finding his interest in marketing while there, accepting a job in New York and, basically, doing well enough at it to retire in a short time.

"But not completely?"

"I'm ready to relax and enjoy life a bit," he answered her question. "But I'm not ready to sit in a corner and rot."

"Why Kansas City?"

"My first major client's corporate offices are here so I visited often and spent quite a bit of time here. I like the slower pace. I like living in the middle of the country. For the most part, within two or three hours, I can be anywhere."

"That's why you chose North KC? So you could be near the airport?"

He nodded.

Autumn glanced at the growing darkness outside and shivered. "Why not someplace warm?"

"I couldn't stand the thought of going somewhere that didn't have four seasons. What would football season be like if it never got cold?"

Her mental image of him lying on the couch crystallized. He'd be watching football. She knew more about him than she had, but he was still an enigma. A very attractive enigma.

He grinned slyly. "You're much easier to talk to when you aren't so tense." He interrupted her thoughts.

"You know, you'd be much easier to talk to if you weren't so...so pushy," she said, at a loss for a better word.

"I think it's called aggressive."

"Call it anything you want," she said. "You're still pushy."

"Trick I learned in New York," he quipped. "And we'd better be going if we're going to have you back at your car when the tow truck gets there."

She didn't prolong her protest that he didn't have to take her when she noticed that it was totally dark outside now. As she gulped down the last of her coffee, which was finally drinking temperature, he got up to get her coat.

"Oh. I forgot to ask," she said as he helped her put it on. "Why were you in my shop yesterday? How did you find me?"

"I suspect the same way you found me,' he answered. "A client of mine, Kevin Anderson—" he paused as she nodded "—brought doughnuts to one of our meetings a couple of weeks ago. On the way home from my printers, I saw your sign and remembered the logo on the doughnut box. Kevin had mentioned your 'unique' cookie bouquets and I was curious. I decided to stop to check them out."

"His wife—"

"Jennifer," he inserted for her.

"—gave me your business card."

"They seem pleased with what I've done for his furniture business."

She laughed. He was finally going to display a smidge of modesty? "Pleased? According to Jen, you walk on water."

He stepped aside with an "after you" gesture toward the elegant foyer. "I haven't demonstrated that skill for them yet. How does she know?"

She was almost past him when she remembered the other thing she meant to ask. She stopped short and he caught her shoulders as he barreled into her.

She was looking back, up. Their lips couldn't have been more than four inches apart. She bit her tongue hard to eradicate the sudden longing for him to kiss her. "Sorry," she said sheepishly, pulling away.

"No problem." His eyes told her he'd rather enjoyed the experience.

"I just remembered the other thing. Why didn't you buy anything?"

He snapped his fingers and hurried past her, calling over his shoulder as he went into his office, "Betty forgot to give you this. Here's my order." He handed her a legal-size sheet of yellow paper as he returned. "I didn't buy anything when I was in the other day because I thought your bouquets would cover a whole lot of bases for me. I wanted to make a list."

She glanced down at the names and delivery addresses as he opened the front door.

"We should have gone through the garage," he mumbled to himself as he stopped beside a numbered pad to punch in the combination that would open the garage door.

"You going to give me a discount?" he asked as he led her to the passenger side and opened the door for her.

"Why should I?"

He went around to his own side and climbed in. "I'm retired, living on a fixed income. It's a large order." She heard him smile in the dark as he listed his reasons. "But probably the most important to you—every one of those names will bring you ten, maybe twenty orders."

"Oh?"

"I'm kidding about the discount," he said, "but I do think you should consider what I'm saying. What's your actual cost for each one of the bouquets? Six, maybe seven dollars?"

She was amazed at how accurate his guess was.

"Your biggest expense is probably the containers, etc., right?"

She nodded, then realized he couldn't see her since he was driving in the dark. "Yes."

"And time, of course. But you have plenty of that now while you're trying to get things going, right?"

"Right."

"So some well-placed bouquets to carefully chosen recipients would be fairly cheap promotion. Where did you say your was car?"

She pointed. "Around that corner. About mid-block. What kind of recipients?"

"Real estate agents, for example. They're always on the lookout for unique gifts to welcome home someone who has bought a house from them. That would be a good start."

A tow truck turned the corner at the other end of the street.

"Is that piece of advice free?" she asked as it pulled up in front of her car, his overhead emergency lights blinking.

This time the garish light painted Brad a sickly yellow and she saw his smile. "Yes."

"Then I'll give you your discount."

He chuckled at her decision. "You learn quickly."

The flashing lights seemed to keep time with her heartbeat. His approval made it feel as if the warm glow was racing along her veins. She retrieved her most businesslike tone. "I noticed you have the delivery addresses here but I didn't see if you listed specific kinds of bouquets."

"Just do something generic. Make them...oh... something special for Valentine's Day?"

"Hearts and flowers?"

"Sounds good." The overhead light came on as he opened his door. "We'd better go talk to the driver," he said.

The light spotlighted the fact that every name on the list was female.

He got out.

"These are all girlfriends?"

"Not quite all of them," he said, leaning down, lounging against his door frame. "I didn't put a few on the list."

The way he'd looked at her, the things he'd said, it had all sounded...felt so...so personal. She'd felt special.

"I thought you said you wanted to get married?" Even as the words popped out, she knew she was out of line. Way out of line.

"I do."

"But..." Her hand fluttered over his list.

"Hey." He lifted his shoulders, amused. "Frogs have to kiss a lot of princesses to find the one who'll turn them into a prince."

She couldn't decide whether to laugh or cry or hit him. That slow half wink, half blink sabotaged all logical thought. Darn it, he was *still* the most attractive man she'd seen in ages. But he had feet of clay, just like the rest of them, after all.

"Don't you think we'd better tell this guy where he should take your car?" he asked.

His "I want to get married" line was absolutely the best line she'd heard in her entire lifetime. She should count herself lucky that he'd chosen to send his "generic" valentines to half the women in the two-state area through her. Shoot, maybe she didn't need his consulting services at all. Maybe all she needed was his business.

"You going to share?" Brad's voice broke into her thoughts. "I'd love to know what is making you smile that way."

No you wouldn't. "I was thinking about Sweet Sensations. I'm feeling very optimistic," she told him.

"Good," he said and turned his attention back to the almost empty freeway. "Not much traffic tonight," he commented.

"I hope you know how much I appreciate you taking me home," she said. "You didn't have to, you know. And I really did plan on riding with the tow truck operator to the garage. After I talked to the mechanic, I was going to call a cab."

"I'd planned to go out soon anyway."

He probably has a date, she thought, suddenly horrified. "Oh, no. I haven't messed up a da...plans you'd made for the evening?" A vivid image of some tall, exquisite beauty named Vanessa—the first name on his list—filled her mind. She could see them, dark heads only inches apart as they leaned across a table, holding hands, candlelight illuminating them and turning their two silhouettes into one flickering shadow on the wall.

"I'd only planned to get something to eat. By myself," he added.

She thought she heard amusement in the last words.

"I'd love company, though. Why don't you join me?"

"I need to get home," she said. "I have to get up outrageously early, you know."

"You also have to eat," he countered smoothly.

But not with you. Seeing this man any more than she had to and for any reason besides business would be absolute stupidity on her part. If she needed proof of that, she only had to remind herself of the extreme disappointment she'd felt when she'd glanced down at his list. From this second on, this was definitely and only a business relationship. And he'd pronounced business hours over so she couldn't even use that for an excuse. "I'd better not."

He shrugged, easily accepting her refusal and she felt crushed all over again. "Can you recommend something close?" he returned to the dinner discussion. "Somewhere I won't feel strange eating alone?"

I'll bet you don't very often. "This is our exit." She pointed at the sign ahead. "What are you in the mood for?"

"Homecooking."

She thought of his wonderful kitchen, of the warm rush she'd felt at her visions of domestic tranquillity. "Maybe you should go home and cook something then."

"I'm a lousy cook," he said. "How do you think my kitchen stays looking so good?"

She smiled as she gave him directions for the next turn.

"Too bad I didn't think of it before we left my side of town. We could have done something at the house."

And *that* sounded dangerous. She laughed out loud. "In other words, you are the classic male chauvinist? A woman's place is in the kitchen?"

"I tasted your cookies and saw you eyeing my kitchen with envy. I'm so good at what I do because I'm good at detecting my client's strengths and skills. My skill is in showing how to emphasize and market them."

"Touché," she said and indicated one final turn.

He suddenly whistled as he shifted down to urge his car up the sharp incline of her father's driveway. "You aren't sure you can afford me?' He leaned forward over the wheel to study the huge house on the small bluff.

She stiffened her spine. "I live with my father." She felt her prim and proper self returning. "He could afford you. That doesn't mean I can."

He pulled to a stop in the circle that skirted the front door and looked around him. Soft, carefully placed landscape lights cast a sheen of wealth over the grounds, making them match the rest of the neighborhood.

"He didn't back your business financially?"

Her short laugh was devoid of humor. "I wish." She immediately felt guilty. "My father is supportive in many, many ways. Financially supporting my 'wild ideas' isn't one of them."

"He didn't want you to do this?" Brad asked.

He had taken the car out of gear, turned in his seat, letting his hand rest on the back of hers. The distance between them seemed greatly reduced. The concern in his face touched a cord with her.

"My father is a very successful businessman. He's letting me live here so I don't have those expenses to worry about. He's given me lots of excellent advice, most of which I've taken. But since his biggest piece of advice was not to start this 'venture'—his word—in the first place—at least not yet—that's about as far as his support goes." She knew she was telling him things she never intended to. "He has, more or less, promised to bail me out when I fail." She forced one more bright smile. "And that's why I came to you. I'm not going to fail." She ruined it by adding, "Am I?"

"Not if I can help it," Brad said and gave her his most sincere, heart-stopping look yet.

The determined set of his strong chin, the quiet assurance in his voice seeped into her, making her feel confident, as if she was going to pull this off after all. The fact that he was taking on her burden made her want to throw herself at his shoulder and cry her eyes out with relief.

"Thanks." She managed to get past the lump in her throat. She fumbled for the door handle, getting out quickly once she had it open. "And thanks for bringing me home," she added, leaning down.

"No problem."

Certain that he wouldn't leave until she was safely inside and just as certain that she would do something really, really foolish if he didn't leave soon, she turned and hurried toward the house.

Five days later, she wasn't feeling quite so kindly toward him. She sat staring at his "order," something she'd taken to doing when she wasn't busy at work—which was most of the time, she thought wryly.

Vanessa
Janet
Lila

Oh, didn't that one stir up visions! And Lila shared Vanessa's delivery address. Autumn's eyes moved up the list and double-checked. If these were all girl-friends, that meant two of them lived—or worked?—under the same roof. Surely, if Brad came to pick one of them up for a date, *that* led to some interesting situations.

Sandra
Sonya

The bell over the door rang and she put the list aside. "May I hel—oh, Dad. What are you up to? Let me get you a cup of coffee."

She came around the end of the counter, moving to the coffee bar quickly so she could ignore the expression he normally wore when he came in. He always looked as if something smelled bad in her shop and she knew that wasn't true. Today, the air was indolent with cinnamon from the rolls she'd just taken from the oven.

"Actually," he said following her, "I'm here on business."

She stopped in the act of reaching for a cup and stared at him. Today, anyway, he was all smiles. "I'd like to order 90 dozen doughnuts, please. I'd like the order divided in thirds and delivered next Wednesday, Thursday and Friday."

She emerged from her stunned silence when he added finally, "What? You aren't going to let me have that cup of coffee now that I'm a customer instead of just your father?"

"Dad."

"Here, let me get *you* some coffee." He reached around her and pulled two of the cups from the stack. Moving her aside gently, he poured from the pot on the warmer beneath the brew basket. "I assume this is fresh?"

She nodded. "I made it only fifteen minutes ago."

He looked around them at the empty store and now his nose wrinkled slightly in the familiar gesture.

"There were several people here at the time," she told him defensively and wished she hadn't bothered. He didn't look as if he believed her anyway. But at least he didn't say she'd probably have to throw the coffee out.

She bit her tongue to keep from explaining once again that her busiest time was usually early in the morning, right before people had to be at work and then at the normal coffee break times. "Why do you want so many doughnuts next week?" she asked, stepping in behind him to follow him to the table.

"I told you about the new digital equipment we've been installing?"

She nodded.

He sat down on one side of the table, placing her cup in front of the opposite chair.

"The company that sold us the equipment is going to send their people next week to train our employees to use them."

His order suddenly made sense. Over a thousand employees worked at his plant, manufacturing the packaging materials he made and distributed worldwide. "So the training sessions will be divided into a third of the employees each day."

He nodded. "I thought it might be a good time to show the employees a little appreciation. I thought of you. I knew I'd have a good excuse to support your business eventually," he added, pleased with himself.

And he'd waited only six months to make that decision, Autumn thought sarcastically. Guilt immediately overwhelmed her. "I do count the doughnuts you've bought for yourself from time to time as support, Dad," she said. "But I also appreciate this order. Thanks."

"I'll have Shanna call you tomorrow to make sure you have all the details." Shanna was his personnel manager. Besides her usual duties, she coordinated employee training or any special events at the plant. She had worked the past twenty years as her father's right-hand "man". Autumn had often wondered why Max Sanderford hadn't married the woman, especially since she'd come into their lives more than four years after Autumn's mother—Max's wife—had taken off. Though he hadn't filed for a divorce by then, he'd known his marriage was over.

She and her father both took sips of their still too hot coffee as they searched for something besides her business to talk about.

"How's your car running now?" Max asked.

"Seems to be fine."

"I'm glad the problem was only a broken timing belt."

"I don't understand exactly what that is, but me, too."

Max started to explain and Autumn held up her hand. "It's okay, Dad. Playing auto mechanic on my own car has never been one of my big dreams. Since the garage knew how to fix it and assured me it isn't likely to happen again soon, I'm happy."

Max chuckled.

"See. I should have been a son. You could have taught him everything you know about cars."

Max shook his head thoughtfully. "I probably wouldn't have had the time anyway."

More sips of coffee.

"So how *are* things here?' Max looked around him, trying to tread lightly on the subject that usually put them at odds with each other while still showing interest.

"Slow, but picking up. Got my first really large order just now," she added with a smile.

He smiled back. "You aren't getting others?"

"Not as big as yours. I had two orders for a couple of dozen doughnuts this morning. I'm getting several of those a week. And I have my first order for more than one cookie bouquet," she added brightly. "That's what I was looking at when you came in."

Her father's lips compressed in a thin, tight line. He managed to push an "Oh" between them.

She wanted him to be excited for her. Brad's order wasn't as large as her father's in volume, but she'd been doing calculations in her head. Brad's final bill would be bigger, even with the discount she planned to give him.

"Twenty-seven cookie bouquets," she said.

"Oh?" He seemed a little more impressed, but then his lip curled in the amazed sneer. "Why would

someone order twenty-seven of them?'' The "them"
came out like a bad word.

"Real estate," she said quickly. "A real estate
company is sending valentine bouquets to the people
who bought houses from them during January." She
hated lying to him. But what could she say? The marketing consultant she'd hired—which her father didn't
know about in the first place and would consider a
waste of valuable resources if he did—was sending
cookie bouquets to his girlfriends?

"Oh." Her father's vocabulary was shrinking. "I'm
still glad you have the bakery part of it to pay the
bills," he muttered as if he couldn't help it.

But it's not paying the bills. She clenched her teeth.
"I still believe the cookie bouquets are going to make
or break me, Dad," she murmured, looking down at
her hands, wondering why she was starting this dead-
end conversation all over again. "Cookie bouquets
are different. Unique. Plain old bakeries are a dime
a dozen."

"But not many of them are owned and operated
by someone with a Masters in Grain Science," he said,
pointedly, for the millionth time.

The pride in his voice was almost amusing. He'd
protested loudly when she'd told him that was her
major. He'd thought she needed an education in
something a bit more traditional. "Well, as you can
see—" she waved her hand to take in the whole shop
"—my customers haven't noticed my degree."

"It's lunchtime." He excused the absence of any
business in her shop and stood, obviously as weary
as she was of going over the same ground again. "So
why don't I take you out to lunch," he offered.

She rose from her chair. "I can't." She looked around them. "I already sent Elaine home."

"You're going to lose—" He broke off, apparently deciding not to start the-abysmal-way-you-treat-your-one-and-only employee discussion again either.

Autumn smiled at him, grateful that she didn't have to rehash and reexplain her and Elaine's agreement. "Thanks, Dad, for the offer of lunch...*and* the order. I'll confirm everything with Shanna tomorrow. Okay?"

"Okay." He picked up the heavy wool dress coat he'd draped over the back of his chair and shrugged into it. She leaned over to brush a kiss against his rough cheek, half expecting him to pull away. Public display of affection was on his list of Rules of Etiquette in the Don't column. Maybe it didn't matter since they were totally alone. "See you tonight?"

He shook his head. "Got a meeting. I'll be home late." He was almost at the door when he snapped his fingers and turned. "Oh, I told Marla not to bother with dinner. Last time she made it when I wasn't going to be home, you didn't eat, either."

Although Max said it without a hint of reprimand, Autumn immediately felt guilty. She promised herself she would leave Marla messages when her plans changed. She often took the housekeeper she so rarely saw anymore for granted.

But the last time she'd missed dinner, she remembered, was the night her car had broken down. Autumn hadn't been the least bit hungry after Brad had brought her home. "I'll manage tonight," she promised her father.

The weather had been unseasonably warm today. She'd been itching to get out and about. Maybe she'd

VAL DANIELS   41

wander down to the Plaza tonight, do some window-shopping, have a nice meal at one of the quieter restaurants.

She watched with pride and affection as Max took his leave. The handsome, self-made executive who was her father got in his appropriately upper-class car and she wished she felt adequate to play the role of Max Sanderford's daughter. She hated not quite fitting in the mold that would have won his unqualified approval. If this bakery *did* prove to be a success, maybe once and for all, she would live up to his expectations, even if she didn't do things exactly the way he thought they should be done.

With a sigh, she freshened her coffee and returned to her stool behind the cash register. And the list. The list that could possibly be the beginning of her success.

CHAPTER THREE

THE MAIN STREET café was busier than Autumn had expected. By the time she was finished with her early dinner, she was glad she'd decided to eat before she wandered around the upscale area that was a gathering place on most weekends. The foyer was packed with diners, waiting to be seated. Trying to get to the front door was like running a gauntlet.

She sidestepped a man's arm as he gestured to make a point to his companion and plowed into someone behind her. Autumn turned to apologize. The polite "sorry" died on her lips.

"Autumn!" Brad Barnett's eyes met hers with a surprised but pleased glint.

"Brad."

All at once, there didn't seem to be a crowd. "Fancy meeting you here," she said and immediately wanted to take back the inane words and replace them with something witty.

He looked over her shoulder, checking, she was certain, to see who she was with. She suddenly felt very alone.

When she'd left home, the idea of an evening on her own—people watching, enjoying the crisp night air, browsing the huge bookstore—just doing exactly what she wanted to do had seemed appealing. For a second, she wished she'd asked one of her college friends to join her. Then she realized he seemed to be alone, too. She felt her grin widen.

Brad answered her smile. "Are you meeting someone?"

"I... No...I..." She waved vaguely toward the door.

"There doesn't seem to be much more room in the bar, Brad." A lovely voice interrupted breathlessly from behind them.

Brad stepped to one side, revealing a woman who was as pretty as her voice. "Oh. You've found a friend in this mob. Aren't you going to introduce us?"

"Vanessa, this is Autumn." Brad performed his duty and seemed to watch her intently.

Vanessa. So this was Vanessa. She looked exactly as Autumn had imagined: tall, willowy, dark, glossy hair and elegant. Nice, too, Autumn thought as the woman extended a warm, wide smile along with beautifully manicured hand.

"Delighted to meet you," Vanessa said. "What a lovely name."

Brad surveyed Autumn with a thoroughness that made her want to check her makeup and comb her hair.

She smiled self-consciously and fingered the wavy hair she'd pulled back in a barrette. "Considering that I could have been Moonbeam or Chastity or Willow—" she shuddered "—it's okay. My mother considered herself a flower child," Autumn said dryly. "Thank heavens, my father insisted on having some say in naming me."

Vanessa's forehead wrinkled. "You mean your mother was a hippie?"

"I'm kind of partial to Chastity," Brad commented with a slow, sexy grin.

Vanessa's laugh was low, throaty. "I'll bet."

And how the heck, Autumn wondered, did he manage to look at her with that seductive gleam in his eyes and not offend his date?

"Would you like to join us?" Brad asked.

Autumn's gaze flew nervously to Vanessa. Did she not know the man had a whole harem? Or did she just put up with all his girlfriends? "I...my...my date went to get the car," she stammered. "We...he had to park a couple of blocks from here."

She bit her lip guiltily as Brad frowned and looked over her head toward the door. It was a little white lie, she excused herself, one meant to save Brad from having to politely include her.

"Brad has this incredible luck," Vanessa was saying. "He drives up to a place and there's a car leaving from right beside the front door. He is the luckiest person I know. I love going places with him for exactly that reason," she added.

Sure. And that's the only reason you go out with him, Autumn thought sarcastically. "I could use a little luck right now," she said. "Maybe some of it will rub off on me."

"I plan to rub a lot on you." His eyelids drooped in a look that would make any normal heart stop beating. Autumn had to concentrate to keep hers going.

No wonder Vanessa was at the top of Brad's list. If you had several dozen girlfriends, it would certainly make things easier if some of them weren't bright enough to notice when you seduced others right in front of you.

"Autumn's my newest client," Brad explained— belatedly Autumn thought.

"If I can afford him," she qualified. "He's working on a proposal for—"

"It's done." He leaned forward. "Betty was going call you in the morning to confirm a time for us to get together," he added, "but I guess that isn't necessary now. About two?" It was a question.

Autumn nodded.

"I'll come by the bakery," he added.

"You own a bakery?" Vanessa asked.

"She makes great doughnuts." Brad looked amused. "And I'll bet she does cakes," he added. "You might want to ask her to do something for Marcia's shower."

Wasn't there a Marcia on the list, too? "What kind of shower?" How did Brad get one girlfriend to agree to give another one a shower?

"It's a baby shower,' Vanessa explained.

Autumn knew her eyes widened as she glanced up at Brad. "Call me. I'll do something really unique for you," She managed to say to Vanessa without choking. Autumn opened her purse to start the search for her business cards.

"Maybe you can give me other recommendations, too? As soon as I told Brad I would do this, I realized I didn't have any idea who to contact or where to go for some of the things I need. I'm new to the area and, until now, he's been less than helpful." Vanessa swivelled a thumb in Brad's direction.

"I'll give her your number later," Brad offered.

"Thanks," Autumn mumbled and looked longingly toward the door.

"I just moved here," Vanessa added with an elegant sigh. Her dark hair swung against her shoulders, catching rich sparks from the soft lighting as she shook her head. "I really don't know if I'll stay." She shot Brad a questioning look.

Maybe Vanessa was waiting for a different kind of offer. One from Brad? Autumn glanced to see his reaction and found him staring at her. Her pulse raced automatically. She felt herself flush.

"Well, it was nice meeting you, Vanessa." She edged a step toward the door. "I have to be... He's probably back with the car by now."

"Barnett, party of two." The loudspeaker overlaid the noise in the large foyer.

Brad took Vanessa's elbow possessively. "Tomorrow," he said to Autumn.

She nodded.

"I'll be in touch in the next day or two about the shower," Vanessa promised. "See, he's already doing an excellent job of marketing for you," she said as if she needed to supply one last testimonial.

"And they're going to give away our table," Brad warned. With a final nod in her direction, he led Vanessa away.

Autumn stared as his tall, dark figure parted the mob as if her were Moses parting the Red Sea. They did make a terrific looking couple, Autumn agreed as the path behind them closed, blocking them from view. Her energy was suddenly gone.

If his marketing talents were anywhere as good as his taste in women, she'd done the right thing in hiring him.

And after meeting Vanessa, how could Autumn sustain a slight belief that Brad might be interested in her, despite the way he acted? She hadn't even seen the other twenty-six.

She fastened her coat and pushed out into the cool night air. Her desire to wander around, doing things alone, was suddenly gone. All she was interested in now was the warm sanctuary of her bedroom at home.

"You've been telling me since I started working here that you weren't interested in any kind of steady relationship. Remember, Autumn," Elaine reminded her the next day as they prepared their first batch of pastries for their early-morning opening. "So why do you care if this guy has one girlfriend or a hundred?"

"I don't know," Autumn said irritably and began to wish she hadn't told her only employee about meeting their new marketing consultant at a restaurant on the Plaza the evening before. "And I'm still not interested. I'm not the type. I don't have time. It wouldn't be practical. It's just..."

"You're interested in him."

Autumn wanted to explain that her insides flip-flopped, every time she saw Brad. She wanted to describe the way her fingers itched and tingled at the thought of touching him.

"But it's silly. My dreams haven't changed, Elaine," she said instead. "I *still* want a national franchise, all the things I've been dreaming about since... since back in college when I first had the idea and started experimenting with the bouquets."

"But now you have to stick to that extensive business plan. Right? And you're afraid you're going to waste all those business and economics classes you took." Elaine's voice was wry. She had a law degree she'd never used.

"My classes didn't do me any more good than yours did," Autumn said, feeling more and more depressed. "If they had, I wouldn't *need* Brad Barnett in the first place."

Elaine pursed her lips. "Surely you don't expect that much of yourself. No one can be an expert in every area. Why should you be as good at marketing as you are at making cookies?"

"Because I'm smarter than everyone else," Autumn quipped.

"Which means you don't need Mr. Macho Barnett," Elaine said pointedly with a chuckle.

"Except his expertise," Autumn acknowledged coolly. "So why is it driving me *so-o-o* crazy that I can't quit thinking about him and all those women?" She suddenly snapped her flour-coated fingers. "Maybe that's it. I thought he was the same type, that neither of us was interested in a permanent commitment. Maybe that's why he fascinated me."

"You may be premature, putting that in the past tense, since he's all you've talked about since the minute we got here."

"Okay, he fascinates me," she admitted. "I thought he might be someone I could . . ." She struggled for a word.

"Have an affair with?" Elaine shook her head. "Sure, Autumn. You're exactly the type. That explains why you've quit going out with the three guys you've dated since I've been working for you. The minute they act halfway like they're interested in a more intimate relationship, you run the other direction."

Autumn lifted her nose. "Maybe I'm becoming more sophisticated. Maybe I'm—"

"And maybe I'm the man in the moon."

Elaine definitely wasn't that. Besides being the perfect mother, wife and part-time employee who had turned into a friend, she definitely wasn't the right sex to be the man in anything. Autumn grinned at her with affection. "You're right. You're the man in the moon. That explains so many things I've never been able to figure out about you."

"And I think you're changing the subject... finally."

"It's about time, don't you think?"

"Except you haven't answered your own question."

"Oh?"

"If you're interested in him because you *aren't* interested in a permanent commitment, why *do* you care if he has 'all those women?'"

It was a question Autumn couldn't answer.

Elaine let her off that hook and put her on another. "How can you afford a marketing consultant?"

Autumn frowned.

"A week ago, you were moaning that you'd gone through so much money for unexpected odds and ends, you were going to have to go out of business a month earlier—you're talking about my job here, remember—than you'd calculated in your original business plan. That gives us four more months."

Elaine knew the trust fund Autumn's grandmother had left her would only finance Sweet Sensations for one year.

"I have to do something," she said. "It's now or never. I thought the phone would ring off the hook with everyone wanting my unique and wonderful bouquets."

Elaine nodded. "Aren't you glad your father suggested the doughnuts and rolls and decorated cakes to help pay the utility bills while people were discovering you?''

Autumn rolled her eyes. "Too bad it hasn't happened that way. And I'd rather spend some of my savings on a little intensive marketing than spend the rest of my life wondering if I didn't give things a fair chance. I'm starting to feel desperate, Elaine. If I have to go out of business two or three months earlier than I planned..." She shrugged. "So be it...at least I'll know I tried."

"There goes my job!" Elaine threw up her hands dramatically. "Your lease is for a year," she added dryly.

"So if this doesn't pan out, we'll both have to get another job. And I'll have to use mine to pay the last few months of my lease. I'll have to get a job anyway if this goes under."

Elaine grimaced in reluctant agreement. "What did your dad say?"

"About hiring Brad, you mean?"

Elaine nodded.

"I haven't told him," she mumbled.

Most of Autumn's friend's thought Max was wonderful. And he was. But they didn't understand how hard it was to let someone you idolized down. Especially when he idolized you back and expected miracles from you. They didn't understand how impossible he made things sometimes. Elaine, who was also fast becoming her best friend, was the only one who seemed to understand.

"I hope I'll soon have something impressive to show him instead."

"So you think Brad can help you turn things around?"

Autumn smiled. "I just hope he's *half* as good as he thinks he is. Sweet Sensations will be on the New York stock exchange by the end of next week."

Elaine laughed, turned back to the huge fryer she was attending and started flipping doughnuts. "I can't wait to see this man."

Elaine was on her way home when Brad came in. She waved to them through the window, then added a thumbs-up for Autumn when Brad's back was turned.

The expensive briefcase he carried clashed with the casual way he was dressed. He had on jeans and a beige sweater. The nondescript color turned his startling eyes a deep blue-green.

Autumn put down the damp cloth she was wiping the top of the counter with and dried her hands. "I'm excited to see what you propose to do for me."

The corner of his mouth tilted in a half smile but he let the opportunity to misinterpret her remark pass without comment. He propped his briefcase on the table closest to the display case. "You close in ten minutes?"

She glanced at the clock behind her.

"Don't let me interrupt you if you have things you have to do. Then, if you want, we can go somewhere and have lunch or coffee while you look this over."

"I know it's silly," she said, feeling her face grow warm, "but even though I close at two, I generally stay around to answer the phone until five. I don't like turning it over to the answering service before then."

He looked at her somberly for a moment, as if he couldn't decide whether he liked being set aside for a phone that might ring. "I like clients who are serious about customer service.'' He jammed the long fingers of one hand into his pocket and hooked his thumb through a belt loop. ''Makes me feel better about marketing their products and gives me one more thing to promote.''

''Let me get you some coffee then.'' She indicated the same table he'd sat at before, inviting him to sit down.

''This is probably better anyway. We won't have to contend with as many interruptions.''

She flushed again, which was really silly. Why should she be embarrassed that he'd guessed there wouldn't be many interruptions to contend with?

Fifteen minutes later, she turned the sign in the window to Closed and joined him.

''Now,'' she said primly, ''tell me your ideas.''

For the next hour, he bounced a variety of suggestions—with a variety of price tags—off her.

''Do you realize you didn't mention the bakery part of your business at all last week when you came to the house?'' he asked as he reached to set some of his papers aside on a nearby table.

''I didn't?'' Autumn fiddled with the sugar packets in the container on the table.

''Does that mean you want me to focus all my energy on the cookie bouquets?''

She knew she was frowning. ''I don't know.'' She hesitated. ''That part of the business has paid more of the bills than . . .'' She suddenly shook her head. ''But that's not what I want to do. I have no intention of spending the rest of my life getting up at four-thirty in the morning to make doughnuts.''

His laugh was low, liquid and held some mysterious note of satisfaction. It sent a chill down her spine that contrarily warmed her.

"Then why are you doing this at all?" The doughnut case earned his "this" gesture. "You'd save a whole lot of money and gain a whole lot of sleep if you did just the bouquets."

"I also wouldn't have a business," she said sharply. "Do you know how many bouquets I've sold in the seven months I've been here?"

She didn't wait for an answer.

"Not counting your order, eleven."

She wished he hadn't mastered the blank, listening stare so well. Though he was probably shocked, his face told her nothing.

"That's an average of less than two a month. My father sent one. Jennifer and Elaine have sent a couple each. I had several orders around Thanksgiving from strangers and I was so excited I had to bite my tongue to keep from giving them away. Then two at Christmas. Two! I'd thought Christmas would be my turning point." She managed to flatten her voice on the last sentence.

"Maybe you've fooled people into thinking you're running a bakery," Brad said.

"But . . . but . . ."

"The best marketing advice I could give you, Autumn, would be to treat your business like what you want it to be. A specialty shop. They are extremely popular right now."

Autumn looked down at the hands she'd clenched in her lap the minute they started discussing the bakery. She stretched her fingers and saw the flour beneath her nails. "I can't give up the bakery."

"Maybe not now," he said. "You've made commitments. I understand that. But think about it. Start checking out different locations for when this lease runs out."

"I can't afford the rent here," she said pointedly.

"That was before you hired me," he said in his arrogant way.

"And what location do you suggest?"

"Westport. The Plaza, maybe."

She shivered internally. Did the man not know how expensive property was in those exclusive areas?

"Maybe even some busy strip shopping center if you prefer to stay in the suburbs," he continued. "Why did you choose this location, anyway?"

"My father helped me find this. It's what I could afford on my budget and he thought the mix of office buildings, with the industrial area nearby would help me build a steady clientele."

"And is that proving to be true?"

"Some. It's growing. There's very little competition."

"Did you ever wonder why?"

She ignored his question. "Before work and break times are steadily getting busier. As people realize I'm here, I think—"

"You'll expand the segment of the business you don't really enjoy?"

She hadn't thought of it like that. She'd only thought of the fact that she would eventually be able to pay the bills. She rose from her chair. She wanted to pace.

Brad stood with her.

"What kind of business is it that your father is in?"

"Manufacturing. His factory makes packaging materials."

"It a whole different thing than retail," he said softly.

For a moment, she felt indignant, defensive of her dad and all the help and advice he'd given her. Then she just felt confused. "So I'm doing *everything* wrong?" She looked up at him. He was standing too close. He was speaking too softly. She cleared her throat and glanced quickly away.

His hand came to cradle her face and turn it gently back toward him. "The very best marketing strategy is finding what you do well, then doing it again and again. You stay away from the things you don't do well."

"You didn't like my doughnuts?" It suddenly seemed very important that he thought her doughnuts were divine.

"I liked them a lot." He smiled. "I misspoke. I should have said you should stay away from things you don't do well or don't like doing. Like you just said, you don't want to spend the rest of your life making doughnuts at four-thirty in the morning. Why would you want to emphasize the aspect of your business you like the least?"

The feel of his fingers where they rested under her chin distracted her to the point she couldn't answer his simple question. She had to put a step between them before she could nod in agreement.

His empty hand dropped to his hip. "You're welcome to make doughnuts in my kitchen anytime you want."

She hadn't noticed that the smile lines on the left side of his mouth disguised and almost hid a small dimple. She felt the urge to examine it. She fisted one hand in the pocket of the smock she wore. "I have my own kitchen." She waved toward the back room. "Industrial strength," she added, "but I suppose that explains why you have such a wonderful kitchen."

He frowned.

"Don't deny that you use it to entice women into your lair." She emphasized each word with an accusing finger.

He laughed. "You forget. This isn't exactly the age of Suzy Homemaker. Most women run in the other direction at the sight of a kitchen." His tone became reflective as he stepped closer again. "You're the only woman who has seemed the least bit impressed with mine so far. Wonder what that means?"

"It means I like to cook." She struggled to sound lighthearted. Damn, those eyes. She loved his eyes. She devoted her attention to studying the color of his sweater but his broad chest distracted her again. "I'll bet you could convince Vanessa to cook something for you in your kitchen," she suggested and wanted to bite off her tongue.

"I already have." His voice was full of amusement.

Why had she said that? Visions Autumn didn't appreciate filled her mind. "That reminds me," she said quickly. "Before you leave, let me go over your order with you. I like to individualize my bouquets a little bit. Maybe you can tell me something about all the . . . each person on your list."

"I assumed you'd do the hearts and flowers routine, like the ones in your book."

"I thought I would, too," she admitted, gaining the courage to look at him again. "But since this is my first valentine season, I hadn't really thought about it until I got your order. If I can think of ways to personalize them, don't you think I should?''

"I think it's an excellent idea." He stepped back over to the table. "So we're going to do the brochures so people can see what you do without actually coming in." He began gathering his things, adding her cookie notebook to the pile of things to put in his briefcase.

"That's why you didn't buy anything that first day?" She'd put two and two together from several things he'd said in the course of their conversation.

"Partly." He smiled. "I was late for an appointment. I'd only stopped to grab a brochure."

"And the other part?"

"I was determined to drink the coffee you forced on me. It irritated me when I burned my tongue." His gaze drifted to her mouth, then back to her eyes. "It reminded me you were a dangerous type and that I should mind my own business," then added, tongue-in-check, "In spite of the fact that you were doing everything wrong."

"How am I dangerous?" Her voice wavered on the edge of disbelieving laughter.

He reached out as if he couldn't resist touching her. "I can tell by the set of this—" his knuckle nudged her chin "—you're determined to go where I've already been."

How did that make her dangerous? She felt her brow wrinkle to frame a million questions she couldn't begin to ask.

"I have real mixed feelings about helping you get there," he answered one of them.

Why? He obviously enjoyed his successes. It was there in every arrogant thing he said. "That really inspires confidence in your proposals," she said dryly. Deep down, she did trust him, she realized. Probably because everything he'd suggested made so much sense.

"Good." He grinned. "Because the feeling that wants you to succeed has been winning the battle. And I'm convinced the options you've chosen are the best ones for you at this point."

As they rehashed some of the specifics, Autumn started to feel optimistic again. But when he got to the part about him writing the marketing letter she would send with the brochure to various businesses, she remembered that he still hadn't said how she would pay him. "You haven't said anything about your fee."

"They're figured into in the prices I quoted you," he explained. "For the volume of business I bring them, I get a large discount at the printers where they'll do your brochure," he added as an example. "The price for the graphic artist who'll design it is in there, too." He suddenly leaned closer. "I also accept gratuities." His lips came a hairsbreadth away, hesitated, then brushed hers lightly.

Before she could respond, as she wanted to, or protest, as she should do, he backed away.

She fingered her lips experimentally and wondered if his tingled as if they'd been shot with electricity.

"Sorry," he apologized, looking away, snapping his briefcase closed with an intensity the action didn't require.

"No problem," she murmured and wished he'd do it again. She wanted time to analyze the sensation that had swept through her in that very brief time when his lips had connected with hers.

"I guess I still like to live dangerously," he added wryly.

That word again.

"Now," he said softly, "get your list so I can give you a rundown on the people I'm sending your bouquets to."

The list was the only reminder she needed to get her brain functioning again. And the names on it were all she needed to convince herself not to take that gentle, heart-stopping kiss too seriously.

CHAPTER FOUR

AUTUMN'S FRUSTRATION level hit an all time high by the time Brad finally left. He took his order and the pen from her. "Go ahead and send the basic valentine bouquet to these." He placed check marks by more than half the names.

"I can surely come up with something unique if you'll just tell me a little abo—"

"I can't think of anything. I really did intend them to be exactly what I ordered—momentos to show I think about them."

Vanessa's name had a check mark, Autumn noticed despite watching him go over the list upside-down.

He told her Marcia was pregnant—which Autumn already knew—and suggested a baby rattle or something similar for hers.

"What if I did the traditional hearts and flowers but decorated the cookies and containers in pinks and blues and with baby shapes and things?" she said enthusiastically.

He made an absentminded but agreeable "hmm" sound.

"It seems that if you were going to have a baby, it wouldn't so much change things as it would put a whole..."

His eyes lifted to hers. One eyebrow arched slightly.

"Different color...or...or slant on the way you saw them," she managed to finish. It was much easier to concentrate when he wasn't concentrating on her.

"Sounds like you've thought about having children. You plan to?"

"Eventually. I want them eventually."

He held her gaze. "When I asked where you'd like Sweet Sensations to be ten years from now, you said you'd like to have franchises in all fifty states." The statement masked a question.

She frowned for a second, then laughed nervously. His expression was too serious. "It's kind of silly to waste time thinking about motherhood when I don't even have a husband."

"You do want one of those, too?"

"Of...of course. Eventually," she added again.

"And you think you'll have more time for a family five or ten years from now? When your business is growing and expanding?" His tone implied that he thought she was delusional.

She shrugged, lifting one shoulder as nonchalantly as she could. "I guess we all have to set our priorities."

His lips compressed in a thoughtful line as he gave her one of his half blinks, almost as if he were dismissing her and the entire conversation. He returned his attention to the list.

The truth was, Autumn found herself wanting to explain, when she'd thought about marriage at all, which wasn't often—she supposed her father's experience with the institution may have colored her perceptions. He'd been married all his life and had acted like a staid and faithful married man, even though he hadn't had a wife around—the images of herself with a husband and children had always been so vague and fuzzy and unreal, marriage seemed remote and distant. In fact, the picture she'd had of Brad on the couch, flipping through the TV channels with the remote control while she puttered in his kitchen had been more vivid and concrete than any marriage fantasy she'd ever had.

Autumn's jaw went lax in surprise. She closed her mouth quickly, relieved to note that he was still engrossed in his order. She denied the thought that she'd been picturing herself married. But the vision *was* the most graphic one she'd ever had, her mind argued. She'd actually seen herself as half of a whole, as part of a couple.

With him!

Brad pointed to the middle of the list and looked up. "Could you do a variety of flowers for this one? Then finish it off with only one heart?"

Autumn nodded, shaking off a kaleidoscope of emotions and praying he couldn't read her mind.

But his smile was pensive as he wrote "flowers" beside that name. "She loves her garden. She mentioned last week how much she misses her flowers."

Her confusion changed to an unwelcome stab of...of...isolation, she decided. She hated being left out. And he certainly wasn't making this part of the process as much fun as she usually had with her orders.

While she struggled to read the name he'd written "flowers" by, Brad hastily penciled in a few different items beside the ones he hadn't checked, telling her nothing about the people who went with the names. On one, he listed a "telephone." The others merely said things like "airplane," "banana," "elephant with trunk raised." He must have a terrific memory, Autumn noted when he handed the list back, because every single item he'd written down had been part of arrangements in her sample book.

"I can do shapes other than what you saw in the examples. Those are just to give customers ideas," she said brightly. "Or maybe we could individualize some of the bouquets with a special message. I can get up to seven words on each cookie, although I usually divide messages longer than three or four words between two." She poised her pen above the first name. Instead of him giving her a "special message" for Vanessa, he extended his hand. She gave the pad back to him.

He frowned as he stared at the list. "Go ahead and do the 'Happy Valentine's Day' bit for these." This time he used quickly scribbled stars. He concentrated on writing specific things beside only two of the recipients. Then he scrawled something in at the bottom of the back page.

When he passed her back the list this time, he stood up. "That'll do it." He suddenly looked impatient with the whole process and anxious to be on his way. He grabbed his navy ski jacket from the back of his chair and shrugged it on while she looked over his chicken scratches to see if she had any questions.

Beside the banana one, he'd said, "Happy Valentine's Day to the Top Banana." Next to Sandra's name, he'd suggested a hot air balloon and the not very original message, "Up, Up and Away." She flipped the sheet over. At the end of the list, he'd added another name, Jolene, complete with a check mark and an asterisk.

Autumn suddenly felt weary. She glanced up at him to find him watching her and reminded herself—yet again—that she was lucky to have his business. Her irritation at his lack of input she excused as disappointment that she wouldn't be able to make the bouquets as spectacular as she would have preferred. But if he was happy...

She plastered on a broad grin. "Well, I guess that takes care of everything."

Everything? his raised brows seemed to ask. The corner of his mouth tipped and displayed the sneaky little dimple. His gaze rested on her lips for a second before he bent his head to zip his jacket. Without looking at her again, he gathered his things.

She went to unlock the door for him. He stopped beside her as she opened it. Momentarily the cocky smile wasn't apparent.

"Oh," she said after a long, silent moment, "I got Betty's message that I could deliver the bouquets next week, but you really don't need to worry. It's my largest order so far, but I don't need to start delivering them a week early to get them out on time."

He shook his head and scowled.

"It isn't a problem," she said. "I can do them in a day. I may deliver a couple the day before, just because they're scattered all over the city, but—"

"It is a problem." He interrupted her, bringing one finger to rest on her lips as he shifted her notebook under his arm. "Remember me telling you all of these orders would bring you more?"

She nodded and his finger strayed to absently push a wayward strand of hair behind her ear. "Delivering them a week ahead of time is my valentine present to *you*."

"Oh." It was all she could say.

His finger returned to outline her bottom lip and it instantly started tingling again. With a slow wink and what Autumn was sure was meant to be a smile—

somehow it seemed sad—he added, "Happy Valentine's Day."

The next day Autumn found herself itchy, on edge and pacing the store.

"What's the matter with you?" Elaine asked her as Autumn passed her for the fortieth time to wipe off and replenish the coffee bar. "That's the third time in five minutes you've gone over there to add one cup to the stack. If it gets any taller, you're going to have to supply a ladder for the customers to reach them."

Autumn glanced over her shoulder sheepishly and removed the top foot from the tower of cups. She opened the cabinet beneath to put them back and decided the whole cabinet probably needed a thorough cleaning. She knelt and began taking things out, moving them to the top of the doughnut case behind her.

"I did that yesterday, Autumn," Elaine said dryly. She stood behind the cash register sipping coffee. "If you aren't pleased with the way I did it, just say so. I'll be glad to do it again."

Autumn dropped her chin to her chest, heaved a huge sigh and began replacing things again. "Don't mind me, Elaine," she said. "For some reason, I'm feeling—" she finally found the right word "—irritable today."

Elaine grimaced good-naturedly. "I noticed. PMS?"

"I wish." Autumn made a face. "At least I'd have a good excuse for feeling this way. I hate it when I'm in—"

The bell above the door dinged and two men came in, interrupting the diatribe Autumn had been ready to launch into.

Elaine waited on them as Autumn sidestepped her and returned to the kitchen. "I'll take care of the apple fritters," she murmured as she passed.

After she put the apple fritters she'd left rising there into the fryer, she stood with her hands on her hips, gazing around her. She'd brought baskets from the storage room for Brad's bouquets. They set on the long stainless-steel counter opposite her, mocking her and waiting for the decorated cookies and tissue paper that would fill them.

By the time she flipped the apple fritters in the hot oil, the bell had dinged six times. She glanced at the clock. A little before ten. Things would be fairly steady for the next half hour or so.

Elaine could handle things. Autumn could keep her grumpy self in the kitchen and out of the way. But when she took the new tray of glazed apple fritters out to put in the case, Autumn got caught up in waiting on a customer while Elaine started a new pot of coffee.

It was nearly eleven o'clock before the place was empty of customers again. Elaine dumped out her cold coffee and poured herself a fresh cup as another woman came in. Autumn motioned her employee to a table. "Go ahead. Take a break. I'll get this."

The woman ordered a cake for her son's birthday the following day. Then she took the last dozen and a half doughnuts back to her office for her fellow employees. Autumn fought the urge to grab them out of her hand and point out that the apple fritters were fresher.

"Whew," Elaine said as Autumn joined her at the table. "If you're not careful, you're going to be a great success."

"Yippee." Autumn groaned and flopped her head down into the cradle her arm made on the table.

"What's the matter, sweetie?" Elaine's tone changed from co-worker/employee to her motherly one. "You should be on top of the world. Our little minirush gets busier and longer every day."

Autumn's "Selling doughnuts and decorated cakes," was muffled.

"The rest will come." Elaine touched her shoulder lightly. "You know, I've been thinking about some of the things you told me that guy—that marketing consultant guy?—said."

Autumn raised her head. "Brad?"

Elaine nodded. "Maybe we should start making one or two of your bouquets again every day for display. If we make them seasonal or generic, we'll sell some of them."

"We tried that. Remember?"

"But those first couple of months, we were lucky to have five to ten customers a day. That's doesn't leave a whole lot of chance you'll get lucky and hit someone at the right time. I'll bet we've had a hundred people in today."

"Ninety-seven." Since day one, Autumn had kept a running tally in her head. She'd always thought she would know she was going to make it when she had an entire week with days back to back that she couldn't keep track of.

"That multiplies your chance of selling a bouquet to someone who needs something at the last minute," Elaine said pointedly. "I'll bet if you would have had a couple out today, you would have sold at least one of them. Besides, all the waste we had were the cookies. We used the stuff in the arrangements again and again.''

Autumn yawned wearily. ''You just like taking the cookies we'd have to throw out home to your kids.''

Elaine tried to look insulted but gave it up and grinned. ''Hey! They've been feeling cheated. They thought it was like winning the lottery when I went to work here and brought home a constant supply of cookies and doughnuts for them after school everyday.''

''If I remember right, you're the one who insisted we start throwing out any leftovers,'' Autumn said dryly.

Another customer came in. Elaine waved at Autumn to remain seated while she got up to help him. He left shortly without buying a thing. ''He wanted doughnuts,'' Elaine explained, rejoining her.

''Figures,'' Autumn said, scowling at the row of fresh apple fritters and the empty pan where the doughnuts had been. ''Maybe I should face reality and get a real job. One with a boss who makes the decisions. When we do have a good day, I can't even judge what we need more of.''

Elaine's eyes widened. ''My, my. We are having a pity-party today.''

''Yeah, and I plan to enjoy it immensely,'' Autumn told her companion.

''When you went to make the apple fritters, we only had two of them left and we still had a tray and a half of doughnuts. How could you have known?'' Elaine pursed her lips primly. ''And this seems like a mighty silly attitude when you've just hired a marketing consultant. You surely don't expect an instant turnaround. Especially when you haven't even put your plans in motion yet."

Autumn glanced up. She'd told Elaine the strategies Brad had suggested and the ones they'd chosen. She hadn't told her about the doubts that left her tossing and turning most nights. The doubts that seemed to come from nowhere.

"Elaine, how in the world did you ever decide not to practice law and become a full-time wife and mother?"

Elaine reared back, her eyes widened. "Whoa! Where'd that come from?"

Autumn grinned. "From a seemingly innocent question Brad asked me yesterday."

"And that was?"

"Well, it wasn't really a question, I guess. I said I planned to have kids eventually and Brad acted like I was expecting a lot if I thought I could have a growing business and a family, too."

Elaine laughed. "It hadn't occurred to you that combining the two might be difficult?"

Autumn shrugged and propped her chin on her fist. "Did you always want to be a wife and mother?"

Elaine nodded.

"More than you wanted to be a lawyer?"

"When I first started law school," Elaine said, "I would have said I wanted them both equally. But I never even considered the idea that I wouldn't marry and have a family. Then I met Jim and when he finally asked me to marry him—" she shook her head, frowning "—well, by then, I guess I could see myself more in that role than I'd ever been able to see myself in some office or courtroom, acting like a lawyer."

"You could have done both."

"Yeah, well, maybe." Elaine made a face. "But I chose the career more or less because my parents were both lawyers and it seemed logical. It wasn't politically correct to say I was there to get my M.R.S. degree. I had to have something to say I was going to do."

"So you don't regret not taking the bar exam?"

Elaine didn't hesitate an instant. "Not a bit." Her smile was pensive. "But there wasn't a thing I *ever* wanted to do more than I wanted to be a mommy. When all my friends were playing with Barbie, I was totally wearing out my baby dolls." She laughed. "Shoot. I was wise before my time. My Dream Barbie is still in its original package, complete with price tag. I guess it's worth a fortune."

"See, you don't need to work at a lousy bakery. Just sell Dream Barbie."

Elaine gave her a horrified look. "Don't say that. I can't believe my luck in finding this job."

And Autumn couldn't believe she'd been fortunate enough to find an employee like Elaine. Smart, dependable and she wasn't concerned about making a lot of money. Jim supported their family comfortably.

Elaine had been frightened of being at loose ends when their youngest daughter started kindergarten in the fall. But was just as concerned about committing to a job. "I'm only applying because the ad said the hours are flexible," she'd told Autumn solemnly the day she'd interviewed. "If that isn't true, don't hire me. My first priority is my family. If the kids are sick or there is something I need to do at school, I expect the time off."

Honest, too.

Autumn had budgeted for an employee for twenty hours a week, simply because her father had been certain she wouldn't be able to hire anyone dependable unless she guaranteed at least that. She'd grinned at Elaine that day and hired her on the spot. They'd been being "flexible" every since. Elaine's willingness to work when she was needed and go home early if she wasn't had saved the business lots of money.

And she actually believed she'd gotten the best end of the deal because, for the first time in eleven years, she'd proudly bought her husband's Christmas present with income she'd earned herself.

They'd definitely established a mutually advantageous, admiration society.

"You'd better not even consider making me give up this job," Elaine was saying. She was interrupted by the ringing phone.

"Guess that means our break is over," Elaine said as Autumn went to answer it.

The voice that washed over her as she picked up the receiver brought back the itchy, irrational, restlessness Elaine's down-to-earth view of life had helped dissipate.

"We may have a problem," Brad said without bothering to identify himself.

"Oh?"

"Who took the pictures for your sample book?" he asked. "A professional photographer?"

She nodded then realized he couldn't see her, though that didn't seem right since his voice brought her a sharp, clear picture of him. "Yes."

"The graphic artist designing your brochure will have it ready to go to the printer tomorrow," he said. "That's the good news. But I just talked to the printer and he reminded me that with the new copyright laws, he won't print the photos without a release from the photographer."

"That shouldn't be a problem." Autumn let go a sigh of relief. "Ryan's a friend. He took them as a favor."

Brad's "good" didn't sound that way, but after a moment he continued. "Could you get it to me by nine tomorrow morning? Maybe you can fax it?"

She did some quick calculations. She'd call Ryan this afternoon, pick up the form—

"Is the release some specific form? How should I get that?"

"He'll have something," Brad said. "In fact, if you call him, you can have him fax it directly to me. You won't even have to pick it up."

Brad had been with a high-powered agency in New York and obviously had every technical wonder invented. Autumn didn't tell him she didn't think Ryan had a fax machine. Shoot. Brad probably thought *she* had a fax machine.

"I'll talk to him this afternoon and pick it up after I leave here," she promised. She'd figure out how to get the form to Brad later. "Was that the only problem?" She shifted from one foot to the other.

"That's it." For a long moment, neither of them said anything. Autumn realized both her hands had clamped around the receiver until her knuckles had turned white. She consciously loosened her grip. "Well . . . then . . ."

"Well then." He mocked, sounding as irritable as she felt. "I'll talk to you later, Autumn," he finally added softly and before she could say goodbye, she heard a click and then the empty line. She hung up the phone, frowning.

When she turned, Elaine stood in front of her with her coat on. "Listen, I was thinking."

"Oh, is that unusual?" Autumn tried to recapture her sense of humor.

"You'd better watch it or I'll change my mind about the offer I'm about to make," Elaine threatened.

Autumn crossed her arms in front of her and waited to hear it.

"It's time for me to pick up Nicki at school," Elaine said, glancing at the clock, "but if you don't mind me also picking up lunch and bringing them both back, let me work this afternoon. You get out of here for while." Elaine motioned toward the phone. "Sounds like you have something you need to do."

"Oh, Elaine, are you sure you wouldn't mind?" A burst of exhilaration fired somewhere in her soul at the thought of a few hours of freedom.

"Listen, it's selfish," Elaine explained, trying to mask her motherly-mode. She lifted a coat-padded shoulder and pulled her stocking cap over her always well-mannered dark hair. "Maybe if you get out of here this afternoon, it will do wonders for that not-PMS mood."

It had done wonders already. Unexplainably exhilarated, Autumn felt like singing and dancing and jumping up and down...till she thought of her father's order.

"What's the matter?" Elaine asked.

"I just remembered. I'd better not. Tomorrow's the first day for the extra thirty dozen doughnut order."

Elaine firmed her chin. "All the more reason for you to get out of here for a little while today. The rest of this week is going to be very busy. Escape while you have the chance. I can mix up the dry ingredients for the doughnuts. Isn't that what you would do if you were here?"

Autumn gnawed at the corner of her lip.

"Don't you trust me?"

"Of course, I do," Autumn reassured her. "But it's my responsibility. You're sure you don't mind?"

"If you're sure you don't mind about Nicki."

All three of Elaine's daughters were well mannered, perfectly behaved and absolutely charming. But the mention of the youngest made Autumn check the clock on the wall behind her. "You'd better get going."

Elaine went, talking all the way out the door. "While I'm gone, write down anything you think of that you need me to do," she called. "Then when Nicki and I get back, you can have the rest of the day off and I'll see you a half hour earlier than usual in the morning. Just like we planned."

Autumn smiled as the door closed behind her friend. The day that had so far been bleak and blustery and cold, suddenly looked much, much brighter.

Autumn had lunch on the go by swinging through a fast-food place. She wasn't sure why. Especially since she had all this unexpected free time. Then she drove directly to Ryan's.

After a much more difficult time than she ever would have guessed—dear friend Ryan made her pay through the nose for the privilege of using his "free" photos the second time—she was on her way again, with the release form.

Stopping by the house, she took a quick shower and pulled her long, wavy mass of unmanageable hair back with a giant bow. Oh, why couldn't she have Elaine's or Vanessa's soft, gleaming dark hair? Why did she have to be stuck with this nondescript-colored lion's mane?

She eyed the thigh length, soft rose sweater she'd paired with her black stretch pants in the mirror. Did she look casual enough to carry off the, "Oh, I was in the neighborhood so I just brought this by," bit? Especially since Brad would know she had to drive an hour just to get to his neighborhood?

She'd say she'd picked up something at the airport for her dad. That was it, she decided. She'd picked something up at the airport.

And since she'd never been good at lying, Autumn stopped, ran in and bought a pack of gum at the airport newsstand before she could gather enough courage to show up on his doorstep.

"This is silly," she muttered on her second time around his block, then forced herself to turn into his driveway.

Her heart fell when she didn't see his car. She couldn't tell if he was home the last time, either, she reminded herself. The garage doors had been closed, just as they were this time. But that time, she'd been there on business.

Business. This *was* business. Neither she nor Ryan had a fax machine and though she could have gone by her father's office and used his, she'd had to pick something up at the airport. *I have every reason in the world for being here.*

That was enough to get her out of the car. She walked calmly to the door. "Business," she murmured. "This is business."

But what excuse would she have to get in? she wondered as her finger hovered over the buzzer. Betty would probably answer so the logical thing to do would be to hand her the release and go home.

But she couldn't.

She needed to see Brad. She wasn't sure why. She just knew she needed to see him.

She would step inside. "Just let me make sure this is the right form," she would say.

And then what if Betty took it, then came back and said he said it was okay?

Or what if Betty just looked at it herself and said she was sure it was all right?

"This is crazy!" Autumn blew at the wisp of bangs on her forehead, straightened her shoulders, set her smile and pushed the doorbell.

It seemed to take forever for anyone to come. Autumn finally heard footsteps on the other side of the heavy door. "Hi," she started to say as it swept inward, but the "*hhh*" was far as she got.

Her mouth had dropped open and she couldn't seem to close it again.

"Oh, hi, Autumn."

"Vanessa," Autumn finally managed.

CHAPTER FIVE

VANESSA DIDN'T SEEM the least surprised to see her. "*Brrrr*," she said, taking hold of Autumn's arm and pulling her inside. She shut the door, closing out the cold.

The day turned a very dark gray again.

"Let me get a light." Vanessa reached past Autumn to flip a switch then wrapped her arms around her shoulders and shivered. "I haven't been out yet today. I didn't realize it was so dreary."

That answered Autumn's unvoiced question. Vanessa had obviously stayed here last night or she wouldn't be able to say she hadn't been out today.

"I...this is just...is Brad around? I won't keep you. He asked for this...." Autumn held out the file folder she'd put the one piece of paper in. "Maybe you could just—"

"You surely have time for a cup of coffee. I'm certain he'll be back fairly soon."

Autumn knew her smile must look sickly.

"I would love some company and a wee bit of pleasant conversation if you have time," Vanessa added.

Put like that, what could Autumn say?

"Let me take your coat." Vanessa helped Autumn take it off. "And this is perfect since I tried calling you a little while ago anyway. Someone told me you were out this afternoon. This will be much better, don't you think?"

Autumn frowned.

"So we can talk about the shower," Vanessa said slowly as if Autumn were dense.

"Oh. The shower. Of course."

Vanessa waved a hand at Brad's office door as she led Autumn past it. "He didn't say when he'd be back and he usually does if he plans to be gone for long, so I expect him anytime," she explained as if she needed to dangle additional incentive for staying.

It worked the opposite way. Autumn halted at the door leading into the dream kitchen. She felt her heart fall. It seemed to be thumping somewhere in the vicinity of her knees and they wavered with a disgusting weakness. With her realization that Vanessa was living with him, Autumn no longer felt an overpowering need to see him. In fact, she felt just the opposite. She needed to escape.

But watching Vanessa bustle around Brad's kitchen as if it were her own ought to be exactly the dose of reality Autumn needed.

This was business, she reminded herself. Bringing the release by. Vanessa's call to Elaine. The baby shower. Business, darn it. And business was the reason she had come here.

Vanessa sighed happily as she led the way to the counter. Waving toward the stools on the opposite side with one hand, she let the other hover near the coffeemaker. "Do you take it black?"

Autumn willed herself to blink. "Sure."

Vanessa poured coffee as Autumn reimprinted the room, complete with the adjacent family room, on her mind. She forcefully implanted Vanessa's image over the one of herself in her fantasy with Brad.

You stay here often? Autumn wanted to ask. She bit her tongue.

"My brother is about to drive me crazy," Vanessa was saying. "He invited me to stay with him while I'm on the waiting list for an apartment, and then he totally ignores me. There are days I think I'm going to go stark-raving mad."

Her frustration with her brother explained why she ended up staying with Brad, Autumn supposed. She focused hard on Vanessa's brother's neglect so she didn't have to think of Vanessa's relationship with Brad. Autumn hadn't experienced sibling relationships personally, but she'd observed lots of them among her friends.

"Brothers do sound like a pain, sometimes," Autumn said, "but I've always envied my friends who had them."

Vanessa placed two cups of coffee on the counter and settled on the stool across from Autumn. "Your friends probably don't have brothers like Brad."

Brad? *Brad* was her brother?

Suddenly Autumn felt so weak, she wasn't sure she'd be able to stay on the tall stool. She gripped the edge of it to make certain. Licking her lips, she grasped for something to say to verify she'd heard Vanessa right. She didn't want to make a total fool of herself. "Probably not," she managed to reply. No one had a brother like Brad. Except Vanessa.

Vanessa stirred milk into her coffee and Autumn allowed the grin she'd been holding in her chest to spread.

"So how much longer will you have to wait for an apartment?" Autumn asked.

"I wish I knew. They said another week and a half at the earliest. It might be another month."

It was in the eyes. The night she'd met Vanessa and thought she looked familiar, she should have looked at her blue eyes. They were exactly the color of Brad's.

"I should have moved in with Gram," Vanessa said.

"Your grandmother?"

Vanessa nodded. "She lives in a garden apartment on the other side of town. It's barely big enough for her and it's one of those where they're connected by intercom to the rest of the complex. I really felt funny about just moving in."

"I can see why you might," Autumn agreed. Her mind was still celebrating the fact that Vanessa was Brad's sister. "And this house is definitely big enough to entertain guests."

"This monstrosity might be part of the problem," Vanessa said wryly. "My brother lets me rattle around here, mostly by myself. Three days a week when Betty is here, it hasn't been bad. But the rest of the time..."

Autumn waited for Vanessa to finish the thought, but two things happened at once: Brad came home and the phone rang.

Vanessa grabbed the receiver from the phone on the built-in desk in the corner, leaving Autumn to greet Brad.

"I guess this explains where you've been," he said, half-smiling, half-serious.

"Was I lost?" she said lightly.

"I stopped by the bakery. Thought I'd save you some trouble since I was in your neck of the woods anyway."

"Guess we had the same idea." Autumn realized how intently she'd focused on him when Vanessa spoke beside them.

"Will you hang up in here?" she asked Brad. "I'm going to take this in your office." The tall woman looked as insubstantial as a feather in the wind.

"Is something wro—" Autumn started to voice her concern.

Brad held up a hand, cautioning her with a slight shake of his head. Vanessa hurried from the room, her head bent.

Autumn turned to exchange glances with Brad and found him at the desk, listening at the receiver. After a second or two when Vanessa must have picked it up in the other room, he set it quietly in its cradle.

Autumn started to get up. "I hope you don't mind but—"

"I'll join you." Brad interrupted with a grin and motioned for her to stay where she was. "We obviously can't go to my office," he added.

Going to the refrigerator, he poured himself a large glass of milk.

"I brought...I had to...bring something to the airport for my father. I thought I might as well go ahead and bring you the release instead of faxing it."

"Thank you. I appreciate the extra effort." He smiled knowingly.

"I...then Vanessa wanted to talk about ordering something for the shower..." They still hadn't gotten around to that subject. That gave her an excuse to stay a little longer, she realized.

"Here." Brad picked up her mug. "I changed my mind. Let's move to the table. We'll be more comfortable."

When he had her settled, she understood why he thought they would be more comfortable. He relaxed—sprawled would be a better description, she decided—stretching full-length across his chair, letting his body and long legs dominate the room. He took a long drink and set the half-empty glass on the table.

"Vanessa and I were going to talk about the shower," she started again nervously.

"Vanessa won't be back for a while."

She frowned at him.

"It's her husband." Brad shot a wry expression at the phone.

"Why wouldn't she come back?"

"Sometimes she goes directly to her room. To cry," he added dryly. "Then she'll come back to rant and rave. She'll be too upset to talk about anything but her problems." He smiled devilishly as something occurred to him. "You can stay and listen for once."

His attitude seemed exactly like the typical brothers Autumn had witnessed over the years.

"Listen to what?"

"She's in the process of getting a divorce. It's been really tough . . . on me," he added with a teasing grin.

Autumn couldn't help but smile. "Why on you?"

"I must have been out of my mind when I said she could come here. I thought it would be a chance for a new start for her, not a renewed opportunity for me to play big brother." His tone was wry, his voice full of frustrated affection. "And since all her friends are in Chicago . . ."

Autumn sipped her coffee, then finished the thought for him. "Big brother has to listen to her problems?"

"Frankly she's driving me crazy."

"So why doesn't she talk to your mother or...or..."

"Mom isn't around."

"Oh?"

"She's in Japan for now," he answered. "She remarried last year. They're on an extended world tour." His expression held fondness.

He got up and warmed her coffee, talking about their family and their growing-up years in Chicago. About their mother's struggles to keep the family together when they lost their small neighborhood grocery store after their father's death when Brad was in his teens. About their grandmother moving to Kansas City ten years ago to remarry.

"She's still in Kansas City?" Autumn asked, remembering that Vanessa had mentioned her, too.

"Yeah." He chuckled. "But she gets as upset as Vanessa. She has these funny, old-fashioned ideas about marriage. She thinks it's forever—not until you decide to leave. She tends to tell Vanessa she's a fool."

"And is she? A fool, I mean?"

He grimaced. "I don't try to figure it out. She says she cares about him but that they've 'drifted apart.'"

He got up to pour himself more milk. When he returned, he brought the coffeepot. Autumn indicated she wanted only half a cup. "If you don't think she'll be back to talk about the shower, I probably should be going." Outside, gathering dusk highlighted barren trees against the pale rose sky. She peered at the clock over the oven. It was almost five-thirty.

Surprise brought her to her feet. "I didn't realize it was getting so late. There's the release," she said, indicating the counter where she'd left the file.

"I saw."

"Would you check and make sure it's o—"

He held up a finger, stopping her. "It's after five." His lowered voice said he had other things in mind after the bewitching hour.

"You weren't here *during* business hours,' she said, ending with a frustrated sigh.

"I didn't know you were going to be." His tone implied he wouldn't have missed her for anything. But the seductive quality seemed too smooth, too automatic, too practiced—just like everything he did. It was one of his business techniques, she told herself.

He set the coffeepot on the table. "Have dinner with me," he said unexpectedly. "We can fix something here or go out if you'd rather. Whatever you'd like."

The dream kitchen tugged on Autumn's every fantasy. "You just don't want to face Vanessa by yourself."

He acknowledged her accusation by spreading his hands in concession. "I'm assuming you wouldn't have driven clear up here to run an errand for your father if you had other plans."

It took a second to remember what he was talking about. Then she remembered the airport. The fact that he'd asked, whatever the reason, meant he didn't have plans, either—

That thought conjured up the long list of female names sitting back on Autumn's desk at the bakery. She couldn't help feeling slightly smug as she mentally crossed off Vanessa's.

That also cleared up the mystery of the double delivery address for the bouquets, Autumn realized with growing satisfaction. Vanessa had intended to stay with Brad's grandmother, Lila. The "Lila" image in

Autumn's imagination suddenly transformed from someone hothouse and exotic to someone warm and sweet, someone who had gray hair and smelled like lilacs.

Autumn smiled.

And even if Brad was looking at her now as if he planned to have her for dessert, with Vanessa here in the house with them, Autumn told herself, she wasn't likely to get...too involved with him.

Autumn avoided his eyes, looking around the kitchen. She set the purse she'd just picked up back on the bar stool where it had been for the past hour. The attraction was his kitchen, Autumn told herself, not him. "All right." She was going to stay. "But let's make something here. I love your kitchen."

One corner of his mouth tilted in a knowing, triumphant grin.

"I do need to call home," Autumn said.

One eyebrow lifted momentarily but he walked over to the phone and lifted the receiver. "Vanessa's still on it," he said, replacing it on the hook. "I suppose you could use the business line in the office, but that's where Vanessa said she was going."

"It can wait," Autumn told him, folding her hands primly in front of her as he went to the freezer and began rummaging around.

"Steaks?" he asked, tossing three frozen packets onto the counter.

"Fine," Autumn agreed.

"Shall we let them thaw a bit?" He didn't wait for an answer. Putting them in the microwave, he pushed a couple of buttons. "This'll get them started."

"I could make some rolls or something while we wait. I have a quick recipe that will rise in the time—"

"Let's relax. Whatever you think, I didn't ask you to stay so you would cook." He smiled and added, "Though it has to be an improvement over me or my sister." He took her hand and led her into the adjoining family room. The jolt his touch sent through Autumn seemed like a warning.

She shouldn't have agreed to this. She'd promised herself only to come here on business. *That was before you found out Vanessa was his sister*, a little voice argued.

No. That was good, common sense, she answered back.

He stopped beside a built-in bar and gestured toward the massive sofa. "Have a seat. Can I get you a drink?" He'd brought his milk with him.

She held up a finger, hurried back to the table and brought back her half-finished coffee. She lifted it to show him. "This is fine. I still..."

He looked at her skeptically.

"...still have to drive home," she resumed. *And I don't trust myself with you for an instant if I let down my guard.*

His sexy wink-blink was followed by a slow smile, suggesting he'd heard the second excuse loud and clear—even if she'd only thought it. Without a drop of alcohol, her head already seemed light.

She was almost disappointed when he sank down at the opposite end of the overstuffed couch and angled himself back into the corner. Her shoulders sagged, releasing tension she hadn't know she felt until it eased.

With one knee curved onto the couch and the other leg stretched in front of him, her original image of him relaxing on the couch alone changed. As he was now, with his arm extended toward her on the back of the seat, there was an inviting, comfortable space for someone to snuggle into.

She fiercely banished a vision of herself in that position from her mind.

"You're what? Twenty-six, twenty-seven years old?" he asked.

"Twenty-six," she confirmed.

"And you still call your father about where you are and what you're doing," Brad asked, turning his glass idly.

Autumn watched the liquid swirl. "I try. Since I live with him, I at least try to let him know whether to wait dinner on me."

"I guess that's logical," Brad agreed, studying her too carefully.

She chewed her lip nervously. "My dad's a wonderful man. He's had to be both my father and my mother. I try to make things as worry-free as possible for him." To survive this, she had to keep the conversation flowing. She babbled about Max always attending every one of her school events, even when it must have been a burden with his ever-growing, demanding business. She told about his struggle to have someone there for her after school so she didn't have to come home from school to an empty house, even when she was older.

"A true saint," Brad said dryly.

"He is," Autumn tried to explain, "but that does makes it difficult sometimes," she added. "Do you have any idea how hard it is when you always fear, at the back of your mind, that you will never be as wonderful as someone else is? That you can't live up to his expectations?''

"Give me an example," he said.

Autumn scowled, trying to think of a good one. "Like my major in college," she finally said.

"Which was?"

"Grain Science."

Brad raised an eyebrow. "Oh?"

She grinned. It was the usual reaction. "He thought I'd totally lost it, that I was going off the deep end and would become a living-off-the-land, free spirit and run off and join some commune like my mother. Whoever has heard of a Grain Science major?" she mimicked his tone.

"I hadn't until just now," he admitted.

"My father wanted to yank me out of Kansas State and send me to Kansas University."

"Why?"

Autumn grinned, tempted to tell him how really bizarre the suggestion had been, especially since K-State was her father's alma mater and KU had always been their biggest rival. He wasn't the least bit fond of the school. Instead she explained that his protests had ended when he discovered that people with degrees in Grain Science usually got great jobs with the major food manufacturers. "Grain Science majors develop most of the new food products in the United States," she added.

"Like?"

"Like all those low-fat cookies and desserts coming on the market now," Autumn said. "Like new varieties of cereals, new, improved cake mixes, drinks, packaged meals and—"

"Okay. I get it." He chuckled and held up his hand. "So why didn't you do that? Go to work for one of them," he clarified.

"Because I guess I'm my father's daughter. I wanted to do something myself. Work hard, be independent. Catch the American dream on my own. Kind of like you," she added.

He let the remark pass without comment but a fleeting expression said it pleased him. "So you're following in his footsteps and he interprets it as following in your mother's?"

Autumn had never been able to put it so concisely. After a moment she nodded. "Don't get me wrong. I love him dearly." She hadn't meant to get into this. She hated her feelings of frustration that she would never measure up to her father. She certainly hadn't intended to discuss her inadequacies with Brad. "He *is* wonderful. I...I just want him to be as proud of me as I am of him. It hurts when I disappoint him."

Brad touched her arm. She was surprised he was so close. She hadn't seen him move. "I envy you having someone around to impress," he said quietly.

Autumn smiled, drawing away just a little, back into her corner of the sofa. "Your family is surely impressed with everything you've done."

"I guess." He leaned forward, propping his elbows on his knees. His hand dangled inches from her leg and Autumn felt its proximity. "It's been convenient for them."

"You've made their life better." It was half statement, half question.

He shrugged and absently traced the edge of the coffee table in front of them. "I've tried. Then sometimes I think..."

''What?''

''Well, like Vanessa. If she didn't have me to run to, she'd still be with Bill, working things out. I'm not sure I've done her a favor.''

''You don't think they should get a divorce?'' He was watching her mouth form every word. It tingled and she resisted the urge to examine it with her finger.

He shook his head. ''I don't know. It isn't my opinion that counts.''

Focusing her attention on her hands, she laced them together in her lap. ''Oh.''

''I try not to analyze human relationships,' he said. ''I think it's important to know what *you* need and want and go after it. Without forcing *your* expectations on other people,'' he added thoughtfully.

Darn it. Now she was doing it. She was watching his lips. ''Wh . . . what do you mean? Is that what Vanessa and Bill are doing?'' Her mouth watered, then seemed excessively dry. ''Forcing their expectations on each other?'' She made herself concentrate on their conversation instead of on him.

''Vanessa is in the same place I am right now.'' He'd leaned back again, closer. His arm rested on the back of the couch, near her shoulder. Idly he twirled one strand of her hair around his finger.

He was making concentration impossible. She tried to remember what they were talking about instead of focusing on the sensations feathering down her neck.

''She's ready to settle down, start a family,'' he continued, reminding her. ''Bill's scared. I can understand that, too. He's on the lower rungs of the management ladder at the company where he works. He wants to go farther. He works all the time. And he wants to be more secure before they have children.

He thinks if he works harder and longer, he'll get ahead faster.''

Brad's subtle cologne overwhelmed Autumn's other senses. She wiggled as far away from him as the arm of the sofa would allow. "So Vanessa left?"

"Vanessa thinks he doesn't care if he ever sees her."

"Oh." Autumn could feel the heat his body generated through the thick material of her sweater.

"But working is Bill's way of dealing with their problems," Brad went on, obviously having no problem at all with his thought processes. "He thinks if he's always at work, he doesn't have to discuss it. Until Vanessa left, he managed to pretend they didn't have one."

"A problem, you mean?"

"Hmm."

She made the mistake of looking at him again. His eyes were still on her mouth and the tip of his tongue dipped out to wet his lip.

She was confused and bemused and, darn it, the man was making her crazy.

She rose quickly, pushing herself away from him. "Maybe we should start dinner," she said. Taking her mug to the kitchen, she placed it in the sink, only to turn and find that he'd followed too closely.

He placed his glass beside her mug. His empty hands settled on either side of her on the counter. "This is nuts," he whispered almost to himself, an irritated edge to the words, "but I'm going to kiss you. I have to."

She froze, dazed. His lips lingered above hers for an infinite second, then covered hers gently.

She stood breathless, paralyzed. He tasted good, warm, sweet. He lifted his head, studied her face. One hand tentatively explored the contours of her jaw. "Damn," he whispered, then kissed her again.

His hand left her face and slid to her back. He drew her close.

She was helpless to stop him, push him away, anything. The breathlessness she felt every time she looked at him culminated in one long sigh as the fingers of his other hand lifted her chin to give him better access to her mouth.

His hand moved to her waist and pressed her against him as his mouthed opened slightly. She followed his lead. Her hands curled against his chest then moved to his back and flattened there.

He touched her lower lip with his tongue, he tasted the other, then moved inside her mouth to leisurely, slowly, sensually explore the sensitive places there.

Her knees grew weak, but his arms surrounded and supported her.

As suddenly as he'd started, he stopped, raising his head. His eyelids looked heavy and she felt his quick heartbeat matching her own. "Damn," he cursed softly, "I want to make love to you, Autumn."

Her heart stopped. It wasn't a question or a request. It was a statement of fact.

Her breath caught in her throat. "Why did you say it like it was a curse?" She'd meant to ask teasingly but the question came out weak, slightly hurt. Her voice was flimsy.

"Because as far as I'm concerned, it is," he answered, then kissed her again.

He raised his head far enough to gasp, then closed the tiny distance he'd let between them. His mouth crushed hers hungrily this time. She responded in kind. Her heart thrummed until she thought it would burst her chest and then she couldn't tell if it was his heart or hers.

With his hands, he methodically explored her back, from her shoulders down, pulling her against him each inch of the way, until she couldn't tell where she left off and he began.

Her body battled for total control of her senses while her mind struggled with his declaration that wanting her was a curse.

Her mind finally won and she managed to bring her hands against his chest, between them. It didn't matter that he'd confirmed that her attraction for him was mutual. It didn't matter that she wanted him more than she'd wanted anything in her life.

"How am I a curse?" she gasped breathlessly.

"Don't remind me. I'd rather pretend you aren't," he murmured, taunting and teasing her lips with tiny nips. His arms tightened around her even as his kiss gentled.

A throat cleared over by the door. "I guess I'm interrupting something," Vanessa said and Autumn finally managed to disengage herself. She groaned inwardly, wondering how she could totally forget that Brad's sister was still in the house with them.

Brad backed away. His hands gripped the counter behind him as he leaned against it.

Vanessa had obviously been crying. Her eyes were red-rimmed. Her nose looked rosy, making the rest of her face seem extremely pale.

"I wondered if you'd take me to the airport, Brad."

Autumn noticed the suitcase on wheels sitting by Vanessa's feet.

She smiled weakly. "Maybe I should just borrow your car? I could call and leave a message, let you know where I park it."

Autumn snapped out of her stupor. "Let me take you," she said. "It isn't much out of the way and I...I need to be going anyway." She looked quickly past Brad. But not quickly enough to miss the challenging quirk of his eyebrows. She concentrated on remembering where she'd put her purse.

From the corner of her eye, she saw him cross his arms over his chest and then cross his ankles as he propped himself against the counter.

"What happened?" Brad asked Vanessa. "Are you going back to him?"

"I don't know." Vanessa's voice held all the confusion and longing that Autumn felt. "I only know neither of us can stand doing this long distance anymore. He's meeting my plane," she ended on a hopeful note.

Autumn had found her things and stood by as Brad gave Vanessa a supportive squeeze. Then he reached in his pocket and pulled out his keys.

In the process of putting on her coat, Autumn froze.

His full attention was on her now. "Stay," he said simply.

Vanessa grabbed the keys and smiled knowingly. "Thanks, Brad. See you later, Autumn?"

Before Autumn could say or do anything else, Brad stepped between them. Autumn heard Vanessa's suitcase wheels, then the opening and closing of the garage door.

Then Brad's expression blocked out everything.

CHAPTER SIX

"RUNNING AWAY?" he asked.

Autumn finished pulling on the second sleeve of her coat. "There's nothing to run away from."

"No?"

She wasn't about to look at him. "Since I'm such a curse, why would you want me to stay anyway?" She reached for the coat's zipper.

"Go ahead. Fasten it. I'm very good with zippers," he said dryly. "But don't expect me to stop once I get started. I tend to get carried away and I might not stop with taking off your coat."

His amusement fueled her irritation but she had to peek at him. "You just want to add another notch to your belt."

That raised one of his eyebrows. "If that's what it takes to get you off my mind, I'll settle for that."

She furiously pulled the zipper to her chin. "I'm not interested in ... in that kind of relationship."

"Neither was I," he said mildly, "but it looks like the only kind you and I are likely to have so, frankly, I've decided I'd settle for sex."

She was suddenly so confused she couldn't think. "You've decided?"

"Yeah." He came two steps closer, within touching distance. Every nerve ending in her body practically screamed with anticipation. And if he touched her again right now, she knew this whole conversation would be academic. No one else had ever made her feel this way. She moved away restlessly, jamming her hands into the pockets of her coat.

"That day in your bakery, the minute you turned on me with that innocent, anxious, eager-to-please gaze, I started fantasizing about whether or not you'd look at me the same way if I got you in my bed. I've never reacted that strongly to a woman—not even when I was fifteen," he added softly. "And my mother used to accuse me of reacting to *every* woman that way then."

His honesty stunned her.

"I came home and started making my order just to have an excuse to come back."

For some inexplicable, ridiculous reason, she felt tears at the back of her eyes. She latched onto his last comment. "You don't really want to send the bouquets?" she asked.

"Dammit. Yes. Of course, I want to send the bouquets."

"Vanessa isn't even here anymore," she muttered inanely.

He dragged one hand through his thick hair, leaving little ridges where his fingers had been.

She clutched the mittens in her pockets as he started to advance on her again.

"Autumn..."

She swiveled and crossed through the archway leading into the family room.

"Autumn?" he said again, close to her ear. "What? Are you just not going to talk to me now?"

"I'm just trying to figure out what you want from me," she said.

"I thought I'd made that very clear," he said so huskily it was almost a growl.

"Sex." She turned, staring up at him, asking for confirmation with her eyes. "That's all?"

"Do I have a choice?"

She frowned.

"What are you willing to give?" He reworded the question.

Her frown turned to a full-fledged scowl.

"That's what I thought," he said when she didn't answer. "What do you see yourself doing three years from now?" It was one of the first questions he'd asked the day she'd come to his office for his marketing help. He asked it in the exact same tone.

Her heart sank as she remembered her answer.

"Shall I tell you what you said?" He compressed his lips momentarily. "You said you saw yourself working twelve-to-fourteen-hour days because you hoped your business would be growing by leaps and bounds."

She looked up at him, startled. "And you asked if that would be all right with me." She shook her head tentatively. "That wasn't one of your usual questions, was it?"

"No," he admitted. "I usually assume if someone comes to me in the first place, they're going to put in the time and effort it takes to succeed. They wouldn't waste my time or their money if they weren't willing to do what it takes." He lodged his thumbs in the belt loops of his jeans.

"And you think I have that?"

His shoulders raised in a shrug. "I believe you have a wonderfully unique product, one that fills a gap in the market. You're enthused and excited about what you're doing. You're anxious—almost overanxious— to please your customers."

A quiet pleasure filled her at his assessment.

"I can't see a reason in the world why you can't have a hundred, two hundred franchises in ten years," he went on. "That's what you said you wanted."

"I said fifty. One in every state."

"When it gets past two or three it won't matter. Busy is busy. Twelve-to-fourteen-hour days are twelve-to-fourteen-hour days."

"I'm not even succeeding with one right now," she reminded him.

"I haven't done my magic yet," he said confidently.

His arrogance never failed to amaze her, but at least he'd given her credit, too. "So how does all this apply to you?" she managed to ask.

"I told you what I want." His hand swept the room in a broad gesture. "I'm ready to concentrate on a family, a wife, a couple of kids. I want to travel. Take them places. I want to work if and when I want to, not because I *have* to to support them."

"Most people do both," she said pointedly. "Have families *and* work."

"I don't want to," he said bluntly. The corner of his mouth twisted slightly. "I saw what that did to my dad."

"You mean his work killed him?"

"I mean that by the *time* it killed him, it hardly mattered. Like you, he was concentrating on building a business. The last couple of years, he was around so seldom, we hardly noticed after he died."

His matter-of-fact tone chilled her.

"We missed the money he'd been bringing home. And of course, he hadn't planned ahead. He had loans everywhere with all his suppliers because every cent he could get his hands on, he'd used to make a down payment on some land—so he could build a second store." He was silent for a moment.

"We lost the land. We couldn't keep up the payments. Mom struggled to save the store but we lost that, too, eventually. We were never able to catch up on what we owed the suppliers."

Autumn wanted to offer comfort, but didn't think he'd accept it, even if she could think of something to say.

His chin lifted proudly. "I worked hard to get where I am. I'll never have to worry about those things happening to me or my family. When I leave this world, I plan to leave a lot more than a financial gap in the lives of the people who are supposed to love me."

She wanted desperately to bring him down a notch or two. Darn it, how could he be so...so...assured, when she didn't know from one day to the next what she might do? "So you've achieved your dreams and don't want a wife who might have some of her own?"

"I want a wife who pursues any dream she wants as long as I'm at the top of her priority list—exactly where I plan to put *her*," he added.

My, my! Mr. Perfection! The sarcastic thought came from her jumble of emotions.

He stalked toward her again. This time, she managed not to back away.

"So you've written me off as wife material. You just want to have sex with me," she said blithely, reminding herself she'd pretty much decided she was interested in the same. She knew now it wasn't true.

"If that's what it takes to get you out of my system." None of their conversation had cooled the heat in his gaze. "Maybe it will get me out of yours, too."

She couldn't boldly wait for him to take her in his arms again. Somehow, it all seemed so cold. She shivered.

"It will be a wonderful experience," he promised in a low seductive voice that washed her in pleasant sensations.

And she didn't doubt him for an instant. She licked her dry lips. "That's exactly *why* I have to be going." She refused to look at him. "I don't want my name added to your list of conquests."

He crossed his arms over his chest. "I don't have a list of conquests."

"Just a valentine order."

"You're jealous?" His chuckle sounded distinctly triumphant.

"I'm not...jealous. I just don't want to be just another name on some macho male's—" she searched for the right word "—hit list." Her chin came up a bit. "But I'll admit, you have the best line I've ever heard. You almost have me convinced I should fall into bed with you."

"How can we get rid of the 'almost'?" He crowded her. "Shall I tell you about my list?"

She hesitated, resenting that if she answered yes, she would confirm his supposition. If she answered no, she might never know the truth.

"You know who Vanessa is," he said pointedly.

Her eyes narrowed. "And that's another thing. Why didn't you introduce her as your sister from the start?"

His gaze held hers. "My sister is a very attractive woman. I liked the way you looked at her that night."

"How'd I look at her?"

"The same way I wanted to look at whomever you were with that night." His lip curled.

She giggled nervously. But she wasn't about to tell him there was no one. "You were jealous?"

"Not jealous." He corrected her. "Just mad as hell."

"Why?"

"At myself," he explained. "Because you weren't with me instead."

The quiet way he said it sobered her again.

"I didn't notice that you had asked me."

"I didn't." His chest heaved with his frustration. "I didn't plan to ever ask you, either." His tone confirmed that his irritation was directed at himself.

She locked her hands in front of her. "So tell me about the rest of your list."

"Lila—the one I wanted flowers for—is my grandmother."

She knew her eyes widened in surprise, giving too much away.

"Marcia is a lifelong friend from our old neighborhood in Chicago. And for the most part, the rest are business contacts."

"For the most part?"

"Okay, they *are* business contacts. Or former ones from back when I worked for the agency in New York."

She managed to smile. "And none of them," she referred back to the names on his list, "are girlfriends?"

"I've gone out with some of them."

"But no longer?"

He lifted a shoulder. "Not unless I need a date for a specific occasion."

"And they don't mind that? Being put aside until you need a date?"

"Not that any of them have said. But they've known I wasn't interested in anything serious or long-term."

"Until now," she reminded him. "You're ready to settle down."

"None of them appeal to me."

"Why?"

"They're not what I'm looking for."

"And neither am I," she said shifting uncomfortably. As much as she wanted to tell him he was wrong, she couldn't.

His mouth pursed. "This is different."

"How? You want a physical relationship because you're attracted to me and then you'll call me when you need a date. If that's different, if that's not being added to your list, then I don't know what is."

He looked as if he wanted to contradict her, but he didn't.

"I'll let you off the hook," she said as brightly as she could. "Now that I know the truth, don't feel obligated to send the bouquets. I'll survive without your business. I've hired Mr. Wizard, remember?"

"I assume this means you aren't planning to take me up on my offer." He looked disappointed but undaunted.

"You shouldn't have given me time to think," she said honestly and wished the wistfulness wasn't there in her voice.

He set his jaw in that determined, arrogant line. "Next time, I won't," he promised.

There won't be a next time, she promised herself.

*   *   *

"I promised you dinner, dammit," he told her minutes later when she insisted it was time for her to go. "You'll have dinner."

But the steaks were still as frozen as when he'd put them into the microwave. "Please. Don't feel obligated."

"We'll go out," he said, heading for the coatrack beside the garage door.

"You have to wait for Vanessa to call," she reminded him and felt immediately guilty. She unzipped her coat and sat primly on the edge of one of the overstuffed chairs in the family room. "I'll wait so I can take you by the airport to pick up your car."

"You don't have to."

"I want to."

With his thumbs in his pockets and one ankle crossed over the other, he propped himself in the archway leading into the kitchen area. "We'll have dinner on the way to the airport to pick up my car."

She gave in gracefully, with a nod.

His gaze fastened on her hungrily. He looked as if he wanted to resume their previous conversation.

"I still need to call my father," she said.

He stepped back from the door, indicating the desk where the phone sat with a sweep of his hand.

She walked stiffly across the room, with him watching her every step of the way. "I just wanted to let you know I won't be home for dinner," she said when the answering machine picked up. With Brad standing only steps away, listening, she was grateful her father wasn't at the other end, asking questions.

With Brad as determined they wouldn't talk business after-hours as she was that she was there for business reasons only, conversation became brittle and forced.

Autumn sighed with relief when Vanessa finally called. The past half hour had felt as if they were fencing. Parry, thrust, sidestep. Parry and sidestep again. She thought she would scream if they had to resort to discussing politics.

"Anyplace in particular you'd like to eat?" he asked as they got into her car a few minutes later.

The thought of spending another hour or two, sitting across a table from him and making small talk almost did her in. "My choice?" she asked brightly.

He nodded. "Sure. Whatever you want."

He didn't even protest when she turned and got into the drive-thru line at a fast-food restaurant. His amused grin acknowledged her slight victory in their nonbattle that felt like some kind of war. "I'm not this cheap," he couldn't resist saying.

"I happen to like cheeseburgers and french fries," she told him airily, then made the mistake of looking at him again.

He was eyeing her with grudging admiration and she immediately remembered the way those lovely, appealing, sensual lips had felt on hers. She glanced away quickly.

Whatever her expression had told him, it seemed to lighten his mood. For the fifteen minutes it took to drive to the airport, he casually handed her the cheeseburger she'd ordered, munched more than his share of the french fries from the giant size he'd offered to share and chatted without the tension that had been so daunting back at his house.

It returned the minute she pulled to a stop behind his car.

"Thanks," he said softly, his hand hesitating on the door handle. His look grazed her lips, then rested there.

"No...no problem."

He opened his mouth to say something, then changed his mind. Instead he leaned across and left a quick kiss on her lips. "Next time," he promised, his jaw firming as he opened his door. "See you soon." His hand lifted in salute.

Autumn let herself breathe again only when she could no longer see him in the rearview mirror.

Four-thirty came far too early the next morning. Elaine was waiting in her car beside the back door of the bakery when Autumn arrived at work. Autumn watched her breath puff out in front of her into the cold morning air as she unlocked the shop.

"You look like hell," Elaine exclaimed as soon as they'd turned on the lights inside.

"What a coincidence," Autumn said. "That's exactly how I feel."

"You're sick?" Elaine's rush of sympathy added guilt to the mix of emotions running around Autumn's head.

"I just didn't sleep well," she said. "Sorry. I didn't mean to snip at you."

"No problem," Elaine said. "I'll make coffee. That should help." By the time she returned with steaming mugs, Autumn had all the equipment turned on and was adding the final ingredients to the first batch of dry ones Elaine had prepared the day before.

They worked steadily for almost an hour in relative silence, then took a break to let the dough they had made into doughnuts and various pastries rise.

"How'd it go yesterday?" Autumn asked as Elaine slumped into the chair beside her and put her feet in the opposite chair.

"Pretty well. Did you check out the receipts?"

Autumn nodded. "Looks like things stayed steady."

"It was," Elaine said. "You did have a visitor, though," she added. Her face was too interested, too alert. "Brad? Your new marketing guy?"

Autumn felt the sudden urge to get busy again. But since she'd just told Elaine the doughnuts needed another half hour, she couldn't think of a single thing to do. And at not quite six in the morning, it wasn't likely the phone would ring or anything else would happen to rescue her. The dark sky had just begun to take on a pink glow at its edge. "Oh?"

"I didn't realize he was such a babe, Autumn. No wonder you hired him."

"I didn't see him before I hired him," Autumn reminded her employee dryly. Well, at least she hadn't known who he was, she amended to herself. "He said he came by to get the release."

"Oh? You talked to him then."

Yeah. I wish talking was all we did. Maybe she wouldn't feel quite so much like she had some kind of crazy hangover this morning. Autumn realized she was rubbing at her lower lip and forced herself to stop. She nodded.

Elaine scowled for a moment. "It seemed like he was here forever," she said. "He came shortly after you left and didn't leave until I closed up. I practically had to kick him out then."

"You didn't tell him I wasn't coming back."

"Sure." She raised a hand in a "who knows" gesture. "I tried anyway. He seemed to think you'd change your mind."

"Oops, guess the secret's out," Autumn said as uncaringly as she could manage. "He's figured out I don't have a life."

Elaine laughed and Autumn felt slightly indignant that she didn't at least try to contradict her.

"Well," Elaine said dreamily, "looking at him definitely made the afternoon pleasant and you should have seen him with Nicki. If the way he wrapped her around his little finger is anything to go by, he's a lady-killer." Her forehead furrowed thoughtfully. "She was totally smitten with him. And he was—oh, I can't explain it—but I swear he's interested in more than a business relationship with you. He just kept hanging around. The look on his face when he finally left . . . Hot damn! And what a catch."

"That cookie bouquet order in there—the one we have to start on this afternoon—is his," Autumn reminded Elaine.

Elaine's mouth fell open. "Oh, yeah. You told me that. I just didn't associate it with . . . oooh, that's not good."

"No kidding," Autumn said. "Like you said, he's a lady-killer. And you ought to hear his line, Elaine. He's good. He explains all those women by saying he's looking for Mrs. Right."

Elaine's gaze was suddenly so intense on her, Autumn squirmed. Darn it! She'd said too much. She bit her tongue belatedly.

"So I'm right? He *is* interested?"

Autumn sat in a frozen stupor for a moment. Interested? Was that the right word to describe mutually raging hormones?

"If you've actually discussed this subject with him, I must be right." Elaine drew her own conclusions. "You must have had a fascinating day yesterday," she prompted. "Come on. Tell. When he left here, he said he might stop by your house."

That revelation seemed to loosen Autumn's tongue. "I don't know if he did or not. I took the release to him."

"At his office?"

"At his home. He works at home."

Elaine's eyebrows raised in misunderstanding.

Autumn's air of indifference turned to a groan. "Oh, Elaine, I don't think Nicki's the only one totally smitten by him."

"That's surely not such a bad thing, especially since you admit he's interested, too," Elaine said.

"It is if it gets me off track," Autumn said.

"How would it get you off track?"

"I can't afford to get caught up in a...in a relationship with someone who wants Suzy Homemaker."

Elaine crossed her arms at her waist and tapped her foot, feigning irritation. "And what's wrong with Suzy Homemaker?"

Autumn laughed as Elaine intended her to, then protested, "You know I admire and respect the choices you've made."

"But you aren't me," Elaine agreed with her usual good humor. "You aren't your father, either, Autumn."

"And what does *that* mean?"

"It means I've been reading too many child psychology books." She did a "just ignore me" wave. "But I do believe most of our self-concept comes from our parents."

Autumn nodded. They'd had these discussions before.

"And you are disciplined, goal-oriented and you see yourself as ultimately successful because that's what your father has taught you to be. Right?"

Autumn couldn't argue but she wasn't sure where this was leading. "And that's bad?"

"Of course it isn't. I hope to teach my daughters exactly the same thing."

"But?"

"The only thing you have to learn, my dear, is not to let anyone else define your idea of success *for* you."

Autumn knew she was scowling.

"What do *you* want, Autumn?" Elaine added quietly. "Just remember that no one can decide that for you—not your father. Not Brad. Not any man—and your definition doesn't always have to stay the same."

Autumn was suddenly stressed and frustrated by the whole conversation. "All I know is what I don't want. I don't want to think about all of this," she said bluntly. "Things are finally taking off a little here. Even straight over-the-counter sales have been better this week than we've ever had. I can practically taste something good coming."

"And we have the two biggest orders we've ever had waiting for us in the kitchen," Elaine added.

Autumn groaned again. "Don't remind me. They're pity-purchases. My father and my marketing consultant."

Elaine pooh-poohed the idea. "If your dad made this order, solely in support of you, why didn't he do it sooner? He could have supplied doughnuts for a coffee break anytime since you started."

Autumn started to interrupt.

Elaine raised a finger to stop her. "Think about it. You know I'm right. He waited until now so he would have a *legitimate* reason to support you. He ran as far in the other direction as he could, just so you *couldn't* accuse him of making a 'pity-purchase,'" she ended disparagingly. "He'd be horrified if he heard you."

"Okay," Autumn agreed. "You're right. I can't have it both ways, can I? I was just griping last week that he'd never bought more than a single doughnut now and again."

Elaine gave her a smug nod. "And what does pity have to do with Brad's order? That's just silly."

"He said it was his valentine present to me."

Elaine opened her mouth then closed it again.

"Don't screw up your face like that, Elaine," Autumn felt compelled to warn, "it may stay that way." She checked the time, then rose. "Come on, let's go fry doughnuts."

"He said what?" Elaine asked, following.

"He told me," Autumn said slowly, "that his order would bring lots more. He said that it was his valentine present to me." She snapped her fingers. "And I'd better call him. As soon as we get this stuff done and we're open, I'd better double-check what we should do about his order."

"Why?"

"When I found out it was a pity-purchase I told him never mind. He never said whether or not I should go ahead with the order." She plopped a couple of doughnuts into the awaiting hot oil and checked to see what Elaine's expression revealed now.

"Well, that must have been an interesting conversation." When Elaine realized Autumn had no intention of expanding on it, she said, "We certainly wouldn't want to miss out if he intends us to go ahead."

"I certainly wouldn't want to hand him a bill and have him say 'I thought you canceled my order,'" Autumn said.

"Yeah, you'll have to call him," Elaine agreed, mixing a new batch of glaze so she could add the finishing touches as soon as Autumn had some of the doughnuts finished.

Autumn put another doughnut on the draining rack and noticed Elaine's smirk. "What?"

"My, my. Aren't we more pleasant and amenable after we come up with an excuse for calling someone we want to call anyway," Elaine mocked her.

"What?"

"Just the idea changed your slant on everything."

Yes, Brad had certainly affected her slant on lots of things, Autumn conceded in her mind. She rolled her eyes and decided to ignore Elaine. "I have no idea what you're talking about."

"You're humming," Elaine started a minute later, adding a chuckle for good measure.

Autumn started to deny it, then realized Elaine was right. She was tempted to throw a hot doughnut at her friend. "And you're going to get fired yet," she retorted instead.

Elaine just grinned. She didn't look a bit worried.

CHAPTER SEVEN

AFTER THEY OPENED, Elaine went to deliver the thirty dozen donuts to the plant and Autumn stayed busy with customers. It was almost eleven by the time Autumn got around to making her call.

She resented her hand shaking as she dialed Brad's number but feeling incensed about it didn't seem to stop it.

The answering service picked it up then transferred her directly to Betty.

"I need to check something on Brad's order," Autumn explained. Elaine hovered and Autumn wished she would have worked the call in while she was gone earlier or waited until Elaine left again to pick up Nicki from school.

"Maybe I can help," Betty offered.

"I...no...well, I don't think so."

"Just a minute, Autumn. I'll see if he's busy."

Autumn thanked her and waited.

A customer came in to occupy Elaine. Autumn sent a silent word of gratitude to him. I'm afraid he'll confirm that I should cancel the order, she excused her nervousness to herself.

"Autumn? Hi, darlin'." He drawled the endearment so easily, Autumn wondered if he used it with all his female clients. But somehow it seemed meant for her. Special. Her heart started the heavy thudding that she should be getting used to. "I was going to call you."

"Oh?"

"When I got back home last night, I realized I didn't thank you properly for running me by the airport to pick up my car."

The kiss was thanks enough, she wanted to say. "I . . . we both had other things on our minds." She wanted to kick herself. What was wrong with a simple "You're welcome," or even "How could I refuse when you brought me clear home after my car broke down?"

"You're right about that."

She heard the teasing note in his voice and managed a half smile. She couldn't tell him most of what they talked about after they'd left the drive-thru restaurant. She only knew whatever it was, it hadn't been as important as her thoughts.

"I know we could have used the time better. I rea—"

"You're telling me."

"I realized this morning that I'm not sure what to do about your order." She ignored his interruption and the innuendo. "I wish I'd clarified this with you last night, but did you still want me to send the cookie bouquets?"

The silence at the other end of the line increased her nervousness.

"Autumn," he said as if she frustrated him greatly, "you put your own interpretation on this order. Of course I want to send them."

"You're not just doing this for me?" She cleared her throat. "Out of pity?"

He paused again. "I do things because I want to. I had this order made up long before I knew there was anything to . . ."

"Pity?"

"That's not my word," he denied abruptly. "I'm glad my order will also show you my support. It's not the same thing at all. I'm always on the lookout for something special to send to my business contacts."

"You are?"

"I pick up things here and there all the time."

"You do?"

"Yes, I do." She heard the amusement return to his voice. "I sent a handy little pocket knife to several of the men on my list a few months ago. I like to let people I work for and with know that I think of them occasionally."

"Oh."

"We're going to one word answers instead of two," he asked dryly.

"Sorry."

"See?"

She searched for something to say that took more than one word. All she could think of was goodbye. "Shall I take Vanessa's bouquet off the order?" she asked, remembering the other thing she'd planned to ask him. "Did you hear from her?"

"She called," he said. "You may as well scratch hers—unless you've thought about how you would deliver them long distance," he amended. "Just add the cost to my bill if you decide to do that."

"She's not coming back?"

"I don't think *she* knows," Brad admitted. "But it definitely won't be right away."

"Well, give her my best wishes," Autumn replied, then remembered the shower. "Does this mean the baby shower has been canceled?"

He laughed. "Oh? All business today, are we?"

She wasn't about to remind him that she and Vanessa had never got around to discussing it.

"Does this mean you're holding our discussion last night against me?" he asked.

She caught her breath. "I never considered holding anything against you."

His voice dipped even lower. "I spent the night wondering how I could have handled things differently and still been honest with you."

She didn't know. She'd wondered herself. "I wish—" And she couldn't say that, either.

He waited for her to finish. "I wish, too," he finally said.

The sound of her heart pounding in her ears was making it impossible to concentrate. "I guess I'd better let you get back to work."

"I'll see you late this afternoon then." This time, he did add a goodbye.

"Wait. This afternoon?"

"Yeah. You still intend to be there until five?"

"Yes. Probably." Her mind was racing. Was he coming by here this afternoon?

"Listen, I'll be tied up at least that late anyway. So you won't have to wait for me, why don't I just come by your house around seven? That will be much better for me."

She was still scrambling for answers.

"Unless you have plans, we'll have that dinner I promised you tonight. We'll go somewhere low-key and you can look this over." He didn't give her much chance to answer. "Okay? I'll pick you up around seven then," he said. "We can discuss the baby shower then, too. Guess I'll be playing host for Marcia."

With that he hung up and Autumn wished with all her heart that she'd been paying attention on their way to pick up his car from the airport.

"Well?" Elaine said practically in her ear as Autumn replaced the phone.

She was so intent on solving Brad's latest puzzle it took her a minute to understand Elaine's question.

"Oh. The bouquets?"

Elaine's rolled her eyes as if she thought Autumn was more than a few cookies short of a dozen.

Autumn told her. "He still wants all of them except one."

"See?" Elaine's smile was smug. "They weren't pity-purchases. They're just like this one." She waved a piece of paper under Autumn's nose. "It's *another* order."

"It is?" Autumn checked to see if they had customers. When she saw the place was empty, she didn't hold back her excitement. "Who?"

"You know the tall blond guy who's in almost every morning?"

Autumn frowned.

"I guess I usually take his money," Elaine said, "so you might not remember him. He has a tattoo on his forearm." Then she negated that description, too. "But I guess you wouldn't have seen it lately. He always has on a scruffy-looking jean jacket."

Autumn no longer cared who he was. "What kind? What kind of bouquet," she added at Elaine's blank stare.

"Valentine. He said he hadn't been going out with his girl long enough to give her jewelry or flowers or anything." Elaine's face contorted with distaste. "He didn't want her to get the wrong idea."

"So which bothers you?" Autumn smiled. "The fact that you've discovered a guy—surprise, surprise—who's afraid of commitment or are you concerned that he insulted my cookies."

"Both, I guess." Elaine's hands found a home on her slender hips. "But as long as he's buying a bouquet, who cares?" The familiar gleam returned to her eyes. "But just between you and me, I hope the girl dumps him the day after she gets it."

"Elaine!" Autumn mocked horror. "Are you saying she won't be pleased with one of my cookie bouquets?"

Elaine looked startled, then guilty. Her protest was half out of her mouth before she realized Autumn was kidding. Her expression instantly changed. "My, my. Aren't we feeling clever?"

"Well, you did say he's one of our regular customers. One doesn't wish bad luck on one's customers."

"Look who's talking," Elaine said primly. "I couldn't read your mind earlier, but I would swear in court that you weren't exactly sending good vibes in the direction of our very best customer so far."

"Then you would be wrong," Autumn said arrogantly.

"Sure. And you want to know the bet I'm making with myself now?"

Autumn looked at her and waited.

"I'm betting that I don't get to deliver these particular bouquets. You're going to come up with some excuse to deliver them yourself."

"You couldn't be more wrong." Autumn did her best not to look as if she'd been caught with her hand in someone else's till.

Elaine shrugged. "I just thought I'd let you know so you didn't have to work so hard at your excuse. I won't be the least surprised or disappointed when you discover you have very important errands to run about the time we're supposed to deliver the first ones tomorrow."

Autumn didn't find it comforting that Elaine had come up with the only excuse she'd been able to think of so far. "Well, I hope it wasn't a major bet," she quipped, "because one of you will definitely lose."

Elaine laughed, exactly as Autumn had intended her to. "Come on," she said. "We'd better get back to work since this will probably be one of our busiest days on record."

For once, Elaine didn't leave until they closed at two.

By the time Autumn went home at five, she had half of Brad's cookies baked and ready for decoration in the morning.

Her three hours alone had given her plenty of time to think and she knew she wasn't going anywhere with Brad that evening.

His honesty had done him in the previous evening. In the wee hours of the morning, he may have figured out what to do differently. And she might not be so lucky tonight.

As much as she liked to pretend otherwise, she knew she couldn't have the kind of relationship Brad had proposed with anyone and come away unscathed. She knew instinctively that with Brad, the damage would be permanent.

Both of them had made their goals perfectly clear. She was nuts if she didn't stick to her guns and only see or talk to him for business reasons. Anything else didn't make sense.

She grimaced. She still hadn't figured out exactly what he was coming for—she couldn't remember a single thing he had mentioned—but if his original plan had been to bring it by the bakery, it could certainly wait until business hours tomorrow. And a business location.

She called the number his service answered before she went home for the day and left a message. "We made a tentative dinner appointment but I remembered another commitment," she told them, "so would you please see that he gets this before six o'clock? I'd hate to have him drive all the way out here for nothing."

She included her father's fax number where he could send the stuff if it couldn't wait and the service promised the message would be delivered promptly.

Her father arrived home about the same time she did. They'd both been going different directions and she hadn't seen him in about three days. "Dad," she greeted him as she got out of her car, surprised at how happy she was to see him.

Max leaned back into his to get his briefcase then looked across the top of his roof. "The doughnuts were a hit," he declared proudly.

"Good. And your meetings? How'd they go?"

He threw his arm around her shoulder as they met in front of his car. "Shanna never fails to amaze me," Max admitted. "She said if we treated the whole thing like a celebration, there would be a lot less grumbling and worry about the changeover. She was right. There was almost an electric excitement all over the plant today." The energy had obviously infected him. There was a little extra bounce in his step as he escorted her up the two steps and into the house.

"Dad? Let's go out to dinner tonight and celebrate ourselves," she suggested.

He grimaced. "I'm exha—"

"Nowhere fancy," she interjected. "Maybe to the barbecue place down the street? We can have a relaxed meal, no interruptions? Just you and me?"

"You don't think we should check and see what Marla left us?" As usual—he'd rarely refused her any reasonable requests—he was weakening.

"We'll leave her a note and she won't have to fix anything for tomorrow night. She'll get a break as her share of our celebration."

He grinned and placed his briefcase on the floor beside the kitchen door. She knew she'd won. "And what are you celebrating?"

"My best day ever," she said. "Your success."

"An evening out with your old man?" His hug was warm and wonderful.

"You've always been my best date," she replied truthfully and tried not to think of the one she'd be missing. Or the man she suspected might change that if she was actually ever stupid enough to go out with him.

"I think I've just been sweet-talked," Max said and looked ready to go back out to the car.

"Let me take a shower," she said, glancing at her watch. They needed to leave around six-thirty. "You'll surely have a much more pleasant time if I don't smell like hot grease."

Max laughed.

"'Bout an hour?"

"That'll give me a chance to read the paper. I'll be in the den when you're ready." She watched as he turned to do exactly what he'd said, bending his head in what she recognized as his moving-on-to-the-next-thing manner. She so wanted to be like him: solid, steady, dependable, yet always moving ahead.

When she rejoined him later, he'd started a fire in the fireplace. She paused in front of it, letting its dry heat penetrate to where her scalp still felt damp. "You ready?"

He looked up from his paper and she almost felt his jolt, even though technically, it was only a slight pause. "You look so much like your mother."

It was her turn to be startled. He rarely referred to the woman who had brought her into the world then immediately deserted both of them.

"Really?"

He nodded.

"Is that good?"

He carefully folded the paper and set it aside. Rising slowly, he grinned. "What do you think got me into trouble in the first place?" With one sweep of his hand he brushed the subject aside and invited her to lead the way. "Let's go eat."

"How do I look like Mom?" she asked as they settled in his luxurious car. Normally, as if by some silent agreement, when her mother was mentioned, the subject was dropped as easily as it came up. Tonight, she didn't like letting it go.

He'd always answered her questions factually, unemotionally. "Your eyes. Your hair." He concentrated on backing out of the garage. "She used to spend hours, ironing her hair, trying to get it as straight as everyone else's."

Autumn watched the corner of his mouth turn up in the dim light from the dashboard.

"Within hours, it would be just as wavy as ever. Exactly like yours."

"She could have kept it," Autumn said dryly.

He patted the ever widening thin spot on the top of his head. "You would have rather had this?"

"I wouldn't have had to worry about it since the gene for baldness comes from the woman's side of the family," she reminded him.

"Since I never met your mother's parents, I don't know if you would have had to worry about this—" he pointed to his head "—if you'd been a boy. But your sons—my grandsons—will."

His reference to her future children sobered her. She wanted to ask, what sons? He'd never once said anything about her having children before.

"Don't you sometimes wish I would have been . . ." she asked as he pulled up to the small restaurant. "A boy, I mean. You've never wished you had a son?"

"Never." The overhead lamp came on as he opened his door. "Well, I guess I should say I've never wished *you* were a boy. If I'd had more than one child, it would've been nice to have a boy. But then again, there are always grandkids."

Second reference in one night. Autumn eyed him strangely.

The smoky scent of burning wood and spicy barbecue sauce filled the night. Max's chest expanded as he filled his lungs with crisp fragrant air. She watched him release it in a long white gust that wavered on the soft breeze, then dissipated around him. "Great idea coming here." He took her arm lightly. "I'm glad you suggested it."

"Me, too."

Conversation stopped until they had ordered at the counter and were seated, then Autumn took up where it had left off. "Why didn't you ever marry again, Dad?"

Max pondered the question. "I guess mostly, I never had time."

"Sometimes I feel guilty, like you thought you couldn't because of me."

"I suppose you are guilty in a way," he said with a grin. "If I didn't have you, I probably would have taken the time. I'm sure I would have wanted a family. I'm not much of a loner but you always seemed like all the family I needed."

"It wasn't bitterness or once bitten, twice shy because of how things turned out with you and Mom?"

"Bitterness and regrets take more time and energy than almost anything else, pumpkin." He called her the affectionate name he'd used when she was a child. She suddenly felt like one again. "I didn't have time for those, either. That's why you have to try so hard not to have regrets. Think about the consequences—"

"Yeah, I know." She raised a hand to stop him.

It had always been his philosophy. She'd heard it so often, she knew it by heart. Think before you act. Then, if you decide to take the action, admit you choose—whether consciously or subconsciously—to accept and handle whatever consequences your actions bring.

"And the thing with my mother was never a regret?"

"How do you think I learned the lesson?" he asked with humor.

"It couldn't have been an easy one."

"You made it easier," he said as their number was called.

When they were elbow deep in barbecue sauce, he looked up at her from the rib he'd been gnawing. "Just out of curiosity, is there a particular reason we were having that conversation?"

She shrugged and licked one finger. "Not really," she answered truthfully. She didn't add that he'd given her plenty of food for thought. "Elaine and I were talking about her family the other day and it just got me thinking."

"About?"

"About whether or not I can do what I want with the business and eventually have a husband and kids, too."

"And you've decided?"

This time, the piece of chicken she was eating received her full attention. "There isn't really anything to decide. As the old saying goes, it takes two to tango."

His grimace of disappointment surprised her.

"You haven't found anyone who makes you feel that old magic yet?"

That surprised her even more. Her father's frankness made her blush.

"Was it there for you and Mom?" She shifted uncomfortably, even as she asked. And a vision of Brad filled her mind and stirred her senses.

Her father laughed. "Like I said earlier, how do you think I got involved with her in the first place?"

"Then you would have taken her back if she ever came back," she said.

"No." His voice was low, grumbly. "At least not after that first couple of years. I'm smart enough to know you can't turn back time. I'm also smart enough to know I could never have forgiven her."

"For hurting you."

"For leaving you motherless," he said simply. "I wouldn't have trusted her again. That would never work." He sighed and picked up his soda. He took a long sip from the straw. "Now," he said, replacing it on the table, "let's talk about something else. Shall we?"

"In a minute." Her hand covered his. "Can I ask you one more thing?"

He looked a little wary. "Sure."

"Why don't you marry Shanna?"

Her question raised both his brows as if the thought had never crossed his mind. Then he smiled. "Maybe I will. Maybe someday I will."

Autumn went to bed shortly after they returned home. Four o'clock was going to come very early again.

It did.

She tripped down the stairs, yawning and blinking, and almost missed the huge envelope her father had placed on the bottom step for her.

She picked it up and read the yellow sticky note he'd attached to the front.

This was in the door when we got home. Sorry I didn't see it before you went to bed. Hope it's nothing too important.

That Brad had come by—despite her canceling their "date"—gave her some satisfaction tinged with a shade of regret. Knowing brought her wide-awake.

Sitting on the step two above where she stood, she opened the packet and read the similar note Brad had posted.

Sorry things didn't work out for you tonight. I brought this by anyway, since we can't go to press without your final approval. Let me know what you think first thing in the morning.

She pulled back one piece of the cardboard that sandwiched a long sheet of paper inside. The brochure! From what she could tell at a glance, the final layout was gorgeous.

She still couldn't remember him saying anything about it the other night, but right now, that didn't matter. His vision was going to help make her business a huge success.

She looked at the clock on the other side of the entryway and grinned. Yeah, he'd love it if she called him first thing in *her* morning.

CHAPTER EIGHT

AUTUMN AND ELAINE both read the brochure carefully in the next couple of hours. By the time Sweet Sensations opened at seven o'clock, Autumn was ready to call Brad and give him the go ahead.

This time, she asked the answering service to put her through instead of leaving a message. Brad answered.

"Autumn." His voice was impersonal.

"Oh, Brad, the brochure looks fantastic," she told him.

"You found it. Good. I'll call and give the printer the go ahead."

"Thank you, I . . . really appreciate you bringing it by."

"I was coming anyway," he reminded her dryly.

"You didn't get my message?"

"I suspected you were hiding out, running away again," he said. "It was worth the trip to find out."

"Brad, I . . ." What could she say? That he was right? That she had been running away? That he was wrong, she'd really had other plans? She gnawed her lower lip.

"Don't worry about it," he said quietly. "To tell the truth, I hadn't mentioned bringing by the final draft of the brochure anyway. I hadn't expected it to be finished so quickly. When Jim called me, it seemed like a good ploy to see you."

She wasn't sure if it was his honesty or his admission that he plotted to see her that made her tongue-tied. "I . . . you . . ."

"I deserved exactly what I got," he said, almost to himself. "I'll learn someday."

"I still appreciate you bringing it by. And since I racked my brain trying to remember what we'd set up, I do appreciate your honesty. I thought I was going crazy."

"Don't worry," he said with a derisive chuckle. "I've promised myself it won't happen again. Look where it got me."

Yeah, look where it got him. Now she was racking her brain again, trying to think of a reason why she might need to meet with him today. She felt the same strange tug she'd felt the other day. "I started your bouquets today." She searched for something to say to distract herself.

"Don't send them, Autumn," he said, interrupting.

His sudden cancellation felt like a gut punch.

"I mean, don't send them today. Wait. Let's do them the first of next week, when we have the brochures. I want you to include at least one with every order. This was my valentine present to you. Remember?"

"But I've already—"

"I have another suggestion. Only this one will cost you," he added. She heard his smile.

Cost her what? Where he was concerned, she wasn't worried about money anymore. In the long run, what he wanted from her now would be much, much more expensive. She no longer believed she could afford him. "Hey, I'm feeling rich," she said nonchalantly, contradicting her thoughts. "I'm having my best week ever."

"Could it be that magical marketing wizard... hmm... what's his name?"

She caught his contagious good spirits. "Brad Barnett?"

"That's him."

She could picture the twinkle in his eyes. "I hate to tell you, but he hasn't done a thing for me yet," she reminded him.

There was a long pause. "Nothing?"

The double-meaning in the words seemed to infuse weakness into her bones. His warm, husky voice seeped through her and left an unfamiliar, heavy yearning behind. She struggled for a teasing, lightness she didn't feel. "He's working on it."

"Yes, I have been," he said determinedly, and he wasn't talking about marketing. He cleared his throat. "But let's get back to business. Let me explain my idea."

Yes. Discussing business was a good idea.

"One of my contacts is helping organize a valentine's charity event for the Heart Association. She called me for a donation."

"Yes?"

"I know this is short notice because it's this Saturday, but I thought of you immediately. Would you consider doing a bigger order for me? Cookie bouquets to use as centerpieces? It's a great opportunity to get your name out there, get some notice."

"How many do they need?"

"That's the catch. They need one for each table. You can start with the ones you were already making for me."

"I can start with . . . ?"

"They need fifty to sixty. At least fifty."

Fifty? By this weekend? And this was Thursday?

"Sure." This was exactly the kind of thing she'd been waiting for. The kind of thing she would have—should have—been looking for, if only she'd met Brad sooner. And these cookies would be the best darn hearts and flowers anyone had ever seen. "Straight valentine bouquets, right? Hearts and flowers?"

"Right."

Her adrenaline was pumping now. Visions of twenty to thirty orders a day for her bouquets danced in her head. And it was a good cause, she thought guiltily. Brad was just doing this out of the goodness of his heart.

"How will people know you donated them, Brad?"

"They'll probably announce it but I know the program will have a donor list." He cleared his throat. "I thought you might go for the idea. I already told them to list Sweet Sensations *and* Barnett Marketing as donors for the centerpieces."

"Then let me really donate," she said. "I'll donate half if you'll donate half."

"You're donating the work" he said.

"Then I'll give them to you half price," she suggested.

"Isn't that the same thing as you donating half?" he pointed out with a laugh.

She saw that slow, sexy half wink in her mind. And she was certain his grin was wider.

"Then make it twenty-five percent off."

"Fair enough," he finally agreed. "What time can you have them done Saturday?"

She did some quick calculations. "Probably by noon. But to be on the safe side, better make it one. Are you going to help me deliver them?" She couldn't even pretend she was still thinking about business.

"Oh, they'll pick them up. Will you be there at one?"

"Yes," she said slowly. "I will be if that's what time you tell them."

"Good. One more thing. You'll go with me Saturday night? I know you'll want to see your handiwork. I also bought tickets."

"I'd...oh, no, I can't," she said. Her shoulders slumped and she knew her heart had fallen as far as her voice.

"Win some. Lose some," he murmured.

"And some get rained out," she concluded for him. It was another of her dad's favorite sayings. "I've already made arrangements for Saturday evening." She tried not to sound disappointed. The Valentine's Ball she was attending with her father had sounded fun when he'd invited her. Now it sounded like a huge bore. "With my father," she added for some mysterious reason. Brad had been honest with her, it suddenly seemed important that she was with him. "That's where I was last night, too. With my father."

For a long moment he was very quiet. "For some reason, I'm becoming very envious of that man."

"And I'm sorry I won't get to see my bouquets," she said.

"I'll take pictures," he promised lightly.

She instantly wondered who he would take in her place at his event. Remembering he only had to start calling the names on his list didn't help dissipate the empty feeling the thought had brought.

"And I guarantee, your cookie bouquets will be a big hit."

"What will they do with them afterward?" she asked.

"Why?" The good humor had returned to his voice. "You don't plan to send them out to fill my order on Monday?"

She forced a laugh. The idea was tempting. "No, your friends will all get fresh cookies," she assured him.

They discussed whether she should put enough cookies in the bouquets for everyone at each table to have one or whether they would be sent home as door prizes. Brad suggested she leave both options open.

"They've sold five hundred tickets and hope to make it to six," he said.

"So I guess I'd better get busy," she said. "I have six hundred cookies to make," she said.

Elaine, who had been hovering for the last couple of minutes, let her mouth fall open.

As soon as Autumn thanked him again for the opportunity, he rang off. Autumn hung up slowly.

"What's the matter?" Elaine asked.

"I'm just doing some calculating." Autumn filled in Elaine on the promise she'd just made. Elaine agreed to come in for part of the day Saturday—not part of their usual bargain—and then went to take care of a customer.

Autumn sighed wearily. She should feel good, she told herself. She'd just made it to Brad's call-when-you-need-a-date-for-a-special-occasion list. She should feel flattered. Instead she felt forlorn.

She didn't have the time for her obsession with the man. She didn't have the energy. And he'd made it clear that she didn't have the right priorities to be considered for his princess list. That exclusive list would hold only one name.

Suddenly it mattered almost more than she could bear that she couldn't be the one name on that list.

Saturday, by the time a middle-aged woman came by to pick up the sixty bouquets—no one had ever given her a final number—it was closer to three-thirty than it was to one and Autumn was exhausted. The last thing she wanted was to dig her one dressy dress and heels out of the closet for the ball she'd promised to attend with her father.

When she arrived home, he came out of his den to greet her. The half-glasses sitting on the middle of his nose indicated that he'd been working himself.

"You're home," he said absently.

"Hi, Dad." She kissed his cheek.

"I thought I'd better let you know, we need to leave about 6:15."

Autumn managed not to groan aloud. "Would it be all right if I wear this?" she teased, waving at her glaze-and-flour-splotched jeans and sweater.

He grinned. "You know I don't care, but I'm afraid you might feel a little out of place." He reached for his back pocket. "Maybe you'd like to go buy something new?"

She stopped him with a hand on his arm. "Dad. You want to leave in only two hours. Do you really think I'd be lucky enough to find something in that time, let alone buy it, get home and get ready?"

He tilted back his head to look at his watch. "Oh. Guess you're right. Well, you know I think you always look great, whatever you wear." Then he scowled.

"You've been putting in some long hours the past couple of days."

"It's that charity thing I told you about," she said.

His face looked blank.

"You know, the centerpieces I donated for some charity fund-raising event tonight?"

His expression changed to one of vague recollection. "Can you afford that?" He asked the same question he'd asked the other night.

She smiled. "Someone else is donating most of the cost, so I'll make out like a bandit on the deal. If I wasn't getting a cent, it would probably be worth it for the exposure." She repeated the answer she'd given him the other night.

But his eyes were already glazing over and she knew his mind was slowly returning to whatever project he'd been working on before she arrived home and interrupted him.

"I'm going to take a shower." She leaned forward to accept his absentminded peck on her cheek. "Maybe I'll have time for a little nap."

Minutes later, she leaned her forehead on the shower wall and let the hot water sluice over her tired back as she tried to think of something to do with her hair.

But her mind kept returning to her father. Her vision of him as she climbed the stairs had been clear. He'd gone back into the den, reached for the basic kitchen timer he always kept at hand, turned it to one hour—or whatever time he needed to quit and get ready for this evening—and immediately became engrossed again in whatever he'd been working on.

As long as she could remember, they'd lived by timers. In a little bit, she'd set one herself to wake her from the short nap she planned to take. Max did not tolerate tardiness. He would expect her to be at the foot of the stairs promptly at the appointed time.

Time reminders, he called them. They'd reminded him when it was time to pick her up from school when she was younger and when he had to quit work to get ready to go to one of her volleyball games. They'd reminded him when it was time to read her a story and get her ready for bed. At work, she knew he used them to remind him when it was time for a meeting or to go to lunch.

She couldn't remember a time when Max hadn't used them. She vividly remembered standing by his big chair in his study, looking up at him as he showed her how to set the first one he'd given her. She couldn't have been more than five or six, just old enough to know her numbers. She could hear his voice, telling her, "I'm putting this on twenty minutes. Now unless you have an emergency, you mustn't bother me again until you hear this go off."

And it had worked. He'd done what he had to do to make a success of his business. And she'd always known she was important. Why else would he have set time aside specifically for her?

She realized she was scrubbing her head a little harder—and longer—than she needed to. Autumn leaned back to let the steamy water rinse the shampoo out of her hair. With her skin already rosy from the heat of the shower, she patted herself dry with the towel instead of rubbing.

Why did she have to go over and over things she wished she'd said to Brad the other evening? Why should she worry about proving to him what her father had proven to her: that having to budget time and energy for someone didn't necessarily mean you weren't a priority.

A priority, a little voice said as she picked up her hairdryer.

Her hand stilled in midair. Brad had said he intended to be *the* priority. The top priority.

Such a slight difference between the words "*a*" and "*the*." And he'd scratched her off his list.

She tried to produce the disdain her thoughts should merit. What sane woman didn't want some kind of life of her own? How dare he...but somehow the indignation wouldn't come. Perhaps because she kept seeing herself as she had been some of those growing up years, sitting on the step, waiting to hear her father's timer go off so she could disturb him.

And trying to picture Brad patiently waiting for her time and attention just didn't work.

Besides, she realized with a dismay that left her physically weak, she was doing exactly the same thing. Didn't Brad's long list of female friends bother her because she wanted to be *his* one and only priority? *The* priority. Half dressed, she sank to the side of the bed.

Maybe it was time that she was honest with *herself*.

Despite everything he'd done and said, even if she was willing to give up the dreams she'd been nurturing for years—which she was *not*—what made her think Brad would choose her to turn him into a prince? Nothing had prepared her for that kind of job. She wasn't equipped. She'd be totally out of her mind to even think along those lines.

Restless, suddenly as cold as ice, she gave up the idea of taking a nap and, instead, used the time to give herself a quickie manicure. As soon as the peach color had dried on her nails, she began working on her wild flyaway hair.

When it was as close to silk as she could get it, she wrapped the mass of it in a tight chignon at the back of her neck and adorned it with a gossamer, glistening white bow.

When her timer went off, she slipped on her heels and paused one more time before her mirror. The time she'd spent had paid off, she decided, lifting her chin. The long length of neck, the slender line of her dress, her for-once-tamed hair, all combined to make her look elegant. Truly elegant.

One thing she could do, and do well when she set her mind to it, was make her father proud. This should do it!

Too bad Brad couldn't see her like this. Then with one more slight twinge of regret that she wasn't going to the charity event with Brad instead of the Valentine's Ball with her father, she promised herself she would mark Brad off *her* list.

The dance was being held at the most lavish hotel in the city. Max and Autumn rode the escalator down to join the crowd outside the ballroom where they were serving cocktails.

"When we went out to dinner the other evening, I wish I would have thought to suggest you bring Shanna tonight," Autumn muttered to Max as the ballroom doors opened and people began filtering into the softly lit room. Over their heads, Autumn could see bright red balloons with long white, pink and silver tails hanging from the ceiling.

"She'll be here," Max told her, a twinkle in his eye.

"Who with?"

"One of our suppliers from out of town. She'd already asked him when I thought to invite her."

Autumn raised an eyebrow. So her father had taken her suggestion seriously. "Oh? You were just going to drop me?"

He chuckled. "Actually I had hoped to bring both my favorite girls. But that wasn't your intention, was it? You were wishing you could wiggle out of this."

If she'd only thought to suggest it sooner, she would be at Brad's function this very minute—admiring her bouquets, she excused the wish—instead of here. "I was wishing I could wiggle out of wearing these heels. I don't think my feet are shaped to fit them anymore."

"That's too bad." He tsk-tsked. "You look fantastic in your finery. You do me proud."

"Thank you, kind sir." She dropped him a hint of a curtsy.

"Let me get you a drink," he suggested, taking a few steps toward the bar. "White wine?"

She nodded. "Maybe that will help."

"He's right," a voice said close to her ear. Even if the low, whipped-cream voice had been disguised, she would have known who it belonged to. There was only one person who could send that shiver down her spine with only two words. Her heart jumped to her throat as she realized Brad's "charity event" was her father's "Valentine's Ball."

She swiveled and found herself almost eye level with Brad. Maybe there were advantages to wearing five-inch heels. She blamed her racing pulse on her surprise at seeing him.

"Don't you think he's a little old for you?"

"He's my father," she protested.

"So you said," he reminded her, "and I'm envious as hell." His gaze slowly made its way down the length of her dark forest green dress. On the return trip, his gaze stopped at the white shawl-like collar that rested low on her arms, baring her neck and shoulders. The fabric draped in a straight line across her breasts, leaving a glimpse of cleavage.

She was getting her wish. He was seeing her this way. She fought the urge to laugh for joy that his event was also hers. And the admiration in his eyes annihilated her earlier resolve to forget about him. She straightened, squaring her shoulders. "You don't look bad yourself."

Understatement. What an incredible understatement! The man could make her drool in blue jeans and a sweater. Now he looked as if he'd just stepped off the cover of a magazine. The black fabric hugged his shoulders, making them look impossibly strong and broad. The stark white shirt highlighted his tan and made his killer smile even more devastating than usual. In this garb, shoot, in any garb— or none—he could do his own pinup calendar and make a fortune.

He took her hand. "Come on. Come see."

She'd gone a few steps with him before she realized her father wouldn't know where to find her.

"I'll watch for him." He read her mind as she hesitated. "But you have to see your bouquets. As the lady in charge told me when I came in, they're exactly the right touch of whimsy."

"What were they going to use before?" Autumn remembered to ask.

"They're very conscientious about using the money they raise for the Heart Association. They were going to sprinkle confetti on the tables."

They stopped in the door leading into the ballroom. Hearts and flowers seemed to blossom everywhere, under wispy clouds of balloons and streamers. She felt her slow smile get wider and wider. It was the first time she'd ever seen them en masse like this, and they were...exactly the right touch of whimsy. Combined with the balloons, they lent the entire room a light-hearted gaiety that seemed to promise a good time ahead for all.

"Ah." She couldn't help her sigh.

"And they will use them as door prizes," he added.

Brad pointed to one corner of the room where buffet tables had been set. "They had four extras. Mrs. Williamson used them there."

She looked up at him, reminding herself she'd crossed him off her list. "Oh, Brad. Thank you for giving me this opportunity."

"I'm just glad you're here to see." His gaze seemed to reflect the stars she felt glowing in her eyes. She couldn't seem to stop them. One of his hands came to cradle her face. He eyed her lips hungrily. "You did a great job."

"Thanks."

With a monumental sigh, he turned back to the foyer. "Come on. I'd better get you back so your father and my date can find us."

His date! Of course. Why hadn't it occurred to her that he wouldn't have come alone? "Of course." Her smile suddenly felt stiff.

He winked, this time intentionally. "Besides, if we walk, I get to see your legs." He referred to the slit up the side of her dress. It came halfway up her thigh and made it possible to negotiate in the long, pencil-straight skirt. "You realize until now, I've never seen your legs?"

She tried to match his light tone. "And?"

His grin grew slightly somber. "I would have been better off not seeing."

Bright red fingernails suddenly closed over his dark sleeve. They both looked behind him to see the body attached to them. "There you are, Brad."

Autumn moved a step to the side to see the woman possessively clinging to his arm more clearly.

"Autumn, this is Miranda."

Another name on his list.

"Miranda, Autumn Sanderford, the woman I was telling you about."

The doll-like petite blonde gave her a plastic smile, almost, but not quite, animating the perfectly featured, exquisitely made-up face. "Oh, the bouquet lady. I can't wait to see them. Brad and Mrs. Williamson tell me they're very impressive." She braced her hand against Brad's arm and raised on tiptoe, trying to see around the group of people cluttering the door.

"You'll see them soon enough," Brad told her, patting the ripe red fingernails and then letting his hand rest over them.

"Well, I'd better find my father," Autumn said, anxious to be away from them. "Nice meeting you, Miranda."

"You, too," Miranda said, but she'd already dismissed her.

She doesn't much like me, Autumn thought and realized she was projecting her own feelings onto Brad's date.

"There you are," Max called, then joined her, bringing Shanna and a jolly looking older man named Carl with him. As soon as the introductions had been made, Autumn explained excitedly that this *was* the event she'd made the centerpieces for. Shanna, the consummate cheerleader, immediately wanted to move into the ballroom so they could see them.

Autumn noticed Brad and Miranda, taking places at a table right in the center of things and steered their party to the side of the room, two rows back and over. "We should be able to carry on a conversation here," she forestalled whatever Shanna started to say as she gestured toward the center of the room. So far, they were the only occupants at the table for ten. "I'll sit here," she said quickly as her father started to pull out a chair facing the crowd.

"You'll see better from this side," Max told her.

"Exactly my point," she told him. "I know what my bouquets look like. It will do me a lot more good if other people can see and admire them."

Max shrugged, but joined her on the side facing the glittery cupids decorating the wall.

"Cupids," Autumn said stupidly. Why hadn't she thought of that for valentine bouquets? Maybe she'd do a few cupids in Brad's bouquets.

"What? What's the matter?"

"I just had an idea for the business," she told Max.

He nodded approvingly. Always thinking of business was something he understood.

Four of the people who had joined their table were a lively group, interested in including all in their friendly fun. For the next hour or so, Autumn managed to ignore the fact that Brad was in the room.

Well, almost. At the buffet, she couldn't help but see that he and Miranda were about ten people up in the long line wandering past the extensive array of food. And once she imagined she heard Miranda laugh—pretty impossible across a crowded room, but it was a practiced laugh that seemed appropriate for the dainty socialite. Then the lights dimmed and the small orchestra began to play and it became much easier to pretend he wasn't sitting over there, less than twenty yards away.

Until he whispered in her ear, sending shimmery jolts up and down her spine. "May I have this dance?"

Max and Shanna were already on the dance floor. Autumn looked at the three other people remaining at the table with her. The salesman who'd come with Shanna had already apologetically explained that he needed to rest and catch his breath. The one couple at the table who had come by themselves were gazing into each other's eyes, continuing to make it obvious that they had no intention of paying any attention to anyone else present.

Autumn turned reluctantly toward him. "What about Miranda?" She strained to look toward the table where they'd been seated, then cursed herself for giving away that she was very aware of where the two of them had sat.

"She's busy." She heard Brad's smile. "Will be for a while," he added. "She was on the committee that put this wingding together. They're preparing to do some of the giveaways and extra fund-raising. So I hoped—" he paused "—I could capture you for at least one dance."

Autumn slipped her feet back into the high heels she'd kicked off under the table and managed not to wince. "I'd love to dance," she lied. Dancing with him was the last thing she wanted to do. It wouldn't help her keep her resolution.

The energetic tune the band had been playing wound to a close as they neared the dance floor. The first notes of the next song were mellow.

Autumn grimaced as she realized if Brad had been thirty seconds later, she could have convinced Carl to dance to this one. She managed to smile as she turned into Brad's arms, stiffening her own to keep him at an impersonal distance.

Brad enfolded her, pulling her close, ignoring her efforts. "You're beautiful," he whispered in her ear.

"Even with this pained look on my face? My feet are killing me." If she could maintain a light tone, maybe it wouldn't matter that she couldn't keep him an arm's length away.

"Then lean on me," Brad said roughly and tightened his hold until she was surprised she could breath. Every thought left her mind as she succumbed to the magic of his arms.

He hummed along with the singer. She felt it as much as she heard him. His low baritone rumbled his chest against hers. The occasional words he sang tickled her ear like a sensual sigh. "I wish I knew all the words," he whispered and she tilted her head back to look up at him.

"You have a nice voice."

"I like music," he confirmed. "Now that I'm retired, I'm going to take some kind of music lessons.

My parents couldn't afford them when I was growing up.''

Autumn felt a guilty stab, remembering the piano lessons her father had sprung for that she hadn't wanted. After two years, her teacher had been the one who finally convinced Max he was wasting his money.

"I took piano lessons," she said. "I wasn't very good.''

A soulful saxophone took over the melodic line of the song. "Maybe I'll try the sax." He smiled then pressed her head back against his shoulder.

He swayed her, surrounded her, overwhelmed her, drawing her impossibly closer, till her whole body seemed to vibrate with a sweet, urgent longing.

How could she cross him off her list when she'd never put him there in the first place? He'd put himself there.

She tilted her head to gaze up at him. He made her laugh. He made her feel good. Strong, kind, generous, determined, he was the man of her dreams she'd never thought to dream of. Until now.

Fascinated, she stroked his smoothly shaved rough cheek with the back of her finger. His gaze caught and held hers, then flared with passion. She stopped breathing and felt her own eyes darken with confusion.

He laughed softly—a cross between a groan of need and a sound of triumph—and she knew she was falling hopelessly in love with him.

Panic stole over her, leaving her trembling. She couldn't find the strength to push herself away. Then he released her, keeping a gentle hold only on her fingertips.

"Let's get out of here," he urged with a growl and lead her toward one of the doors in the side of the big ballroom.

Even as she reminded herself she had no business going anywhere with him, her legs followed.

CHAPTER NINE

"Autumn."

Her father's voice stopped her cold. She wasn't sure whether Brad intended to release her fingers or whether her sudden halt pulled them from his grasp. All she knew was that she came out of her daze and her brain began to function again. He was here with a date. She hadn't even thought of her father.

Max was smiling. "I haven't met your friend," he said. "I assume you know each other well?"

He'd obviously seen them dancing. Autumn knew her face was red to the roots of her hair. "Dad, this is my... friend, Brad Barnett. Brad, my father, Max Sanderford."

After a second's hesitation, Brad extended his hand. "Nice to meet you, Mr. Sanderford," he said. His other hand went to the small of her back and rested there possessively, starting the quiet, confusing, needy sensations all over again.

"A friend from college?" Max questioned as they exchanged the mandatory handshake.

"We met through business," Autumn inserted quickly. "He comes into the bakery from time to time."

She felt Brad's eyes on her and shifted from one foot to the other. Her feet suddenly hurt again. But Brad didn't correct the impression she'd given her father.

"Oh? You work in that area?"

"I'm a consultant. I work all over the city—when I work."

Her father's eyebrows raised at the last words.

"He's worked hard enough that he has the luxury of not working at all if he so chooses," Autumn explained, aware for the first time that her father had also had that option for several years. But he'd never taken it.

She was suddenly anxious for this whole conversation to end. She looked up at Brad. "Well, thank you for the dance, Brad." She stepped away from him, toward her father.

For a moment, she thought he would protest. Instead he dipped his head. "My pleasure." His eyes crackled with the opposite.

The lights, which had been dimmed for dancing, gradually came up to brilliant, making the world real again. Careful not to look directly at Brad, Autumn made a weak joke. "Looks like they want to make sure we can find our way back to our tables."

Max nodded once more to Brad and then led the way back to their table. By the time they got there, Max was brimming with curiosity. "Seems like a nice enough guy," Max said then explained to Shanna and those sitting with them that he had just met one of Autumn's friends. "What kind of consulting does he—"

Autumn raised her hand. "They're ready to give away the raffle prizes," she said. "Where are the extra tickets you bought, Dad?"

Max leaned back to fish the wad of tickets the committee had been selling all evening from his pant's pocket.

"First," Mrs. Williamson, the chairman of the event, said from behind the microphone, "if you'll notice, each place at the tables has been numbered. Miranda, my assistant this year—please could you give her a hand for the wonderful job she has done?" When the polite applause died, Mrs. Williamson continued as if she'd never interrupted herself. "Miranda is going to draw a number from one to ten."

Miranda drew a small bit of paper from the bowl Mrs. Williamson held.

"The number is three," Mrs. Williamson said. "Those of you lucky enough to be occupying position number three at each table—" she paused for effect "—get to take home the charming edible centerpieces."

There was an audible murmur of appreciation from the various "threes." At her table, Autumn looked to see that the man who'd barely taken his eyes off his date had won her bouquet. He didn't show signs of noticing his good fortune now until Shanna leaned across and congratulated him.

"Or, of course, you are welcome to share the cookies with your table mates," Mrs. Williamson said, then tittered at what she obviously thought a witty remark.

"Mr. Brad Barnett, owner of Barnett Marketing and Ms. Autumn Sanderford, owner of Sweet Sensations, generously donated the lovely centerpieces. Would you please stand?" she added without further ado. "In honor of the Heart Association, the cause we're here to promote, Ms. Sanderford assures me that the cookies are low fat and have no cholesterol."

Max touched the back of her chair to pull it out for her. Autumn rose self-consciously, her eyes going immediately to Brad.

Autumn felt as much as saw Max's raised eyebrows. Brad's courtly nod in her direction seemed excessively formal. Autumn thankfully sank back into her seat.

The flutter of applause drowned her father's comment to her and she leaned closer to his mouth. "He's a marketing consultant." He asked, "You've hired a marketing consultant?"

She was sure her nod was barely perceptible to anyone else at the table. But Max received it loud and clear.

"It was an impulse," she said, licking her lips. "I thought you'd say I couldn't afford him—not that I can—but it was too late since I'd already—"

"And has he done your business any good?" he said, interrupting her.

She shrugged. "It's too early to tell." She finally met his eyes and realized the disapproval she'd anticipated wasn't there. Maybe he was a little hurt that she didn't seek his advise. "We've really only started." She waved toward the centerpiece. "This is the first suggestion we've had time to put into motion yet. But I've ordered some nice brochures. They're at the printers now. That's what was in the package in the door the other night," she added, then smiled at him hopefully. "They're going to be impressive, Dad."

"I'll look forward to seeing them," he said evenly.

Shanna leaned over her companion and took the raffle tickets from Autumn's fist. "How are you two going to know if you win anything or not?" she explained as Mrs. Williamson and Miranda continued to call out numbers from the podium. After every two or three, they'd introduce another donor and make them stand.

Autumn glanced at Max's profile. It seemed awfully somber. When her gaze turned almost wistfully to Brad's, his looked exactly the same.

He ambushed her as she was on her way back from the powder room a little later. His grim expression hadn't changed but he managed to tilt one corner of his mouth. "You should have warned me," he said dryly.

She frowned.

"That you don't want to share credit for your success."

The frown changed to a full-fledged scowl.

"You should have told me. I would have made sure only Sweet Sensations was promoted as a donor. I don't need the publicity."

"I don't understand."

"You didn't introduce me as your marketing consultant. Frankly I didn't understand why until you looked so crushed when Mrs. Williamson gave away the game."

She laughed, suddenly comprehending. Her reaction seemed to darken his already foul mood. "You mean I didn't introduce you that way to my father? I hadn't told him I'd hired you. I didn't want . . . I was afraid he wouldn't approve," she tried to explain.

That didn't seem to help, either. But something clicked in that busy brain of his. She could almost visualize the wheels turning. "And that's what you're doing, isn't it?"

"What?"

"You don't care about making yourself happy. Just as long as you please him."

"And is there something wrong with that?"

"There is if you make yourself—and everyone else—miserable."

"I'm not miserable."

"Not yet."

"And you're just worried about you," she accused, her voice rising in disbelief. "You're jealous of my father?"

His jaw tightened and a muscle jumped into prominence there. "Jealous as hell," he said between clenched teeth.

"That's sick," she said.

"I know," he agreed.

She didn't know whether to laugh or cry. He didn't give her the chance to do either.

"I thought I was competing with a some half-baked idea—"

"Half-baked? You think my business is half-baked?" She wanted to hit him. She managed to fist her hands on her waist instead.

"I didn't say business. I said *idea*. I'm talking about your future plans. Where's the passion?"

He could have used any word but that.

"It's there now," he said as if he enjoyed pointing it out. "Now that you're angry, those hazel eyes are snapping sparks at me, and that face..." He raked his hand through his hair, leaving little ridges running from his forehead to his nape. "It's there when you talk about your bouquets," he added in a monotone. "Your eyes light. You get excited. Elaine told me you spend your afternoons in that kitchen, experimenting with recipes and designs and decorating. She said you thrive on the creation. You won't even let her touch the cookies for the bouquets except for taking them in and out of the oven. Why are you trying so hard to bury that side of yourself?''

Autumn opened her mouth to defend herself.

"Then every time I question you on your future plans," he went on, "you answer in a monotone, as if you've been practicing some scripted thing you've memorized but don't care about. Who are you trying to impress? Your father?''

She sputtered.

And his voice softened. "You were ashamed to tell him you'd hired me. Why?''

"I told you . . . he . . . I didn't think he'd approve.''

"And his approval is all that matters?''

"Yes. No. I don't know," she moaned.

He took her hand and drew her past the ballroom, down a dimly lit corridor by empty meeting rooms to a small alcove filled with plants. He pulled her into it, into the shadows and into his arms.

His hands framed her face and he groaned. "How can you do this to me?''

"Do what?" she managed to ask as his lips softly touched hers.

"Convince me I've finally found the woman I've been looking for and then turn out to be all wrong.'' His lips sipped at hers, robbing her of breath before he shared his.

How could this be wrong? She tried to ask it and he kissed the words away, into oblivion.

"You *are* a curse," Brad said on a gasp before he deepened the kiss.

Autumn responded eagerly—much to her despair. She wanted to strike out at him, as he'd done to her.

Her wounds were open and raw. But his touch numbed the pain as he pulled her closer, as if he would make her a part of him if he could.

It was Brad who finally put her away from him.

She stood her ground, panting as she struggled for equilibrium.

He licked his lips and tugged gently at a strand of hair that had escaped and fallen across her cheek. "I like it down," he said. "Wild. You look like an ice maiden with it sleeked back like that. I've wanted to rip that comb out since you got here."

"It's a barrette," she said inanely. "And I hate my hair." The world was starting to stabilize and the pain was returning. She sucked in a deep breath. "I'm sorry if you think I don't appreciate what you're doing for me."

"You're paying me. I don't mind. You missed the point," he murmured.

Disregarding his commentary, she continued. "I truly, truly, don't mind sharing the spotlight or giving credit where credit is due. It's just that—" she chewed at the corner of her lip "—so far, I've taken lots of Dad's advice. When I haven't, it's been awkward."

"He wouldn't have approved?"

"I thought he would say I was wasting my money."

"And did he?"

"I think he was hurt. Especially finding out that way." That sobered her again. "I should have told him in the beginning." She realized they weren't getting anywhere with this discussion and shook her head. "So if that isn't the problem, what is? I'm still not sure."

"My problem is you," he said bluntly, crossing his arms over his chest. "I've never felt more like a prince than when I've kissed you."

She couldn't help but smile. "You surely don't expect me to believe you've felt like a poor, ugly frog all your life," she protested. "And I'll bet that line has gotten you more women than you can count."

"I've never used it before," he denied.

She laughed, displaying skepticism even though, deep down, the knowledge grew that he would always tell her the absolute truth.

"It hasn't done me a lot of good with you."

More than you'll know. She'd come closer to throwing caution to the wind, to giving in to her inclinations and damning the consequences than with any other man in her entire life. "You said you liked people who know what they want." She lifted her chin. "All I know is, you're a distraction that might keep me from getting what I want."

"That's the problem. You *don't* know." As if he couldn't help it, his hands came back to her bare shoulders.

Electricity charged though her and she backed away, into a potted plant.

He caught her then dropped his hands to his sides.

She wasn't going to argue with him. She wasn't sure anymore. "And do you know what *you* want?"

He nodded. "And what I don't want. I don't want to be going through what Vanessa is, five years from now."

Autumn bit her lip again. "And you won't have to if you have everything on your own terms."

He nodded again. "That's how it works. And now I understand I'm not just competing with your cookie bouquets, I can move on. It'll make it much easier to give you up.''

"I'm not yours to give up,'' she said. ''Would you at least explain why it's so bad to want my father's approval?''

He looked at her sadly. ''It isn't. Unless that's your motivation for the goals you set and everything you do.''

"If that were true, why am I doing what I'm doing? Dad thought I should go for the secure thing and work for some big food manufacturing business.''

"Why didn't you?''

"I wanted to make cookie bouquets,'' she said simply.

"So your concession to him is turning *that* into big business.''

The light dawned. She realized he was right. The cookie bouquets had been hers. The bakery had been her father's. How could a business remain small and intimate yet still enjoy long-term, continued success had been his question; franchises had been her answer.

"At least I'm willing to make concessions,'' she argued. ''You're so determined not to follow in your father's footsteps, you're not willing to make any. You don't need a wife, Mr. Barnett. What you need is a puppet.''

She saw his jaw tighten. It gave her little satisfaction that she'd struck home a blow of her own. ''Whew,'' she said, wiping her brow with the back of her hand. ''That was close. There for a minute, I considered making concessions for you, too. And what would I be getting?''

She didn't wait for a reply since, for once, he looked speechless. She stepped out from the shadowed alcove, into the muted light of the hall. "You just made me realize I already have one man in my life who makes me practically crazy trying to gain his approval. I don't need another."

With that, she swiveled on her heels. She wished the floors of the corridor weren't covered with carpet. She needed to hear the determined *tap*, *tap* as she walked away from him. Maybe it would cover the sound of her heart cracking in umpteen places.

"Autumn?"

She kept walking. "Thanks for the education, Brad," she called over her shoulder. "Close call."

Max was hovering in the brightly lit foyer of the ballroom. He came toward her worriedly as she entered. "Autumn, my dear, what happened to you? I've been loo—"

"Can we go home, Dad," she asked flatly.

He glanced at his watch.

"Please?"

She saw his gaze catch on something behind her. "I'll go tell Shanna," he said softly.

"Let me get the car," she begged him and he quickly handed her the receipt for the valet parking.

He disappeared into the ballroom.

She kept walking.

Bright and early Monday morning, Autumn and Elaine started Brad's valentine bouquets. By mid-morning a third of them—the ones going to the north side of town—were ready to be delivered.

"So are you going to let me deliver them?" Elaine asked.

Autumn mustered a smile. "Tell your schizophrenic friend that you win the bet," she said, tossing Elaine her coat from the hook by the back door.

"I promise a detailed report," Elaine teased as the phone rang.

Autumn froze. "Would you mind getting that before you leave?" she said, wiggling her fingers. "I have to get some of this stickiness off my hands before I touch anything."

Elaine reappeared a minute later and rehung her coat on the hook. "That was Brad," she said. "If I wait just a little, we should have the brochures. He said someone from the printers will be bringing them by shortly."

Autumn realized she was holding her breath and let out a sigh.

Elaine leaned over the stainless-steel counter and propped her hands on her fists. "You want to tell me what's going on now?"

"What do you mean?"

Elaine rolled her eyes. "Well for starters," she drawled, "you look like you haven't slept for a week. You jump every time the phone rings. You haven't said more than two words all morning—"

"We've been busy," Autumn exclaimed.

"—and you'd already washed your hands twice before the phone rang. I haven't seen you touch a thing that could have made them dirty since the last time."

The bell over the door rang and Autumn straightened then hesitated.

Elaine reached behind her and pushed the swinging doors open an inch. "It's safe," she said wryly. "It's just a customer."

Autumn pushed past her and hoped the you're-out-of-your-mind look she threw her companion was halfway believable. She prayed the new brochures would come soon.

The delivery man brought them just as the last of a string of customers was leaving twenty minutes later.

"We'll talk this afternoon," Elaine promised on her final trip in to carry the last of the bouquets to her car.

"I'll look forward to it," Autumn called sweetly as she removed another tray of cookies from the oven, then went to take care of yet another customer.

By the time Elaine returned it was almost one in the afternoon.

"You got Nicki from school okay?" Autumn asked as soon as she walked in.

"I made it back with five minutes to spare," Elaine said as she started to take off her coat.

"Don't do that," Autumn cautioned her. "I have another six ready to go. Except for one that's a little out of your way, they all go to this side of town. You may as well take them on your way home, don't you think?"

Elaine looked at her knowingly. "You don't even want a report on the deliveries I made this morning."

"I can wait," Autumn said. "Maybe if you regale me with the details in the morning, it will help keep me awake."

Elaine didn't say a word. Just shook her head and started the process of carrying bouquets to her station wagon again.

The next morning went about the same, except they took orders for several additional bouquets.

"Must be that thing Saturday night," Elaine thought aloud as she hung up from taking the fifth order.

"That's what I would guess."

"You don't seem too thrilled about it," Elaine commented as she tied giant bows around the woven wicker baskets Autumn had finished arranging cookies in.

"I am."

"I just can't tell, huh?" Elaine propped herself against the counter and watched Autumn put the finishing touches on the bouquet she was working on for Marcia. "That's going to be cute," she commented on the pink and blue baby booties Autumn had just decorated the heart shaped cookie with.

She stepped back to admire her new design: valentine bouquet for a pregnant lady. "Thanks."

"Are you ever going to tell me what happened over the weekend?"

"I don't know," Autumn answered, wiping frosting from her fingers on the damp cloth she kept close at hand. Setting the six cookies she'd just finished aside to dry, she gathered some of the cupids and arrowed hearts she'd perfected yesterday. Slicking on the white frosting that would be the base for her final decorations, she referred to Brad's list. This one was for Miranda.

She winced, as if an arrow made from cookie dough could actually prick and cause her pain. Stripping off her plastic gloves, she went into the bathroom to get a tissue.

"Hey, you aren't crying, are you?" Elaine came closer and touched her arm.

"I think I'm catching a cold."

"Come on, babe, tell me what happened. What's made you so quiet and subdued?"

Autumn sniffed once, washed and gloved her hands again and went back to work. These cookies would be glitzy and glamorous, to match the woman who would receive them. "Can you believe," she managed to say despite the giant clog in her throat, "that someone would name some blond, blue-eyed Barbie doll, Miranda?"

"You've seen her?" Elaine's interest was definitely piqued. "And the rest of them? What'd you do? Check them out over the weekend? That would explain why you look like you haven't slept in days and why you're not interested in any of the deliveries I've made so far."

"I saw Miranda," Autumn admitted, mixing red, glittery sugar bits into a glob of the bright red frosting they'd made in quantity. She explained about the dance, about seeing the bouquets they'd worked so hard on the previous week. "Miranda was there with Brad," she finished, taking a deep breath. Because she had the momentum going, she couldn't seem to help adding, "I realized I've fallen in love with him."

"Oh, Autumn—" Elaine started in a joyous voice, then tempered the enthusiasm as Autumn glanced up and caught her eye. "I take it that's not good," she said weakly.

"I'll get over it," Autumn said flatly.

"Oh, Autumn." This time, Elaine's tone held remorse and sympathy. "You shouldn't have to. He seemed so...so...perfect for you."

"He was. He is," she said. "The problem is me. I'm not perfect for him. And for the first time in my life, I sort of understand why my mother probably left.''

"Why?" Elaine looked stunned.

"I'm not faulting my father," Autumn quickly said, adding that her father had spent all day Sunday out somewhere with Shanna. "But I suddenly realized how much of my life I've spent, trying to live up to his expectations and please him. If my mother was as imperfect as I am, it must have been very frustrating."

"What does that have to do with Brad?" Elaine asked.

Autumn shrugged, she hoped nonchalantly. "Brad is like my dad. He's genuinely nice, ambitious, strong, confident—"

Elaine held up her hands. "I get the picture. I don't need a list of his qualifications."

"He has very specific ideas about what he wants for the rest of his life. I'm still fumbling. The thought of trying to live up to his expectations terrifies me. I refuse to try."

"Does he want you to?" Elaine asked gently.

Autumn nodded. "I think so."

"Does he love you?"

"I don't know." The cookie she'd just finished elaborately decorating crumbled in her hand.

Elaine hurried to get one of the extras they'd made to replace it. "You forgot one of his qualities. He wants you only if you'll reshape your life to conform with what he wants? That sounds so selfish."

"How is it selfish to know what you want and go after it?" Autumn said defending him. "I admire people like that. *You're* like that." She gave her friend a smile. "I want to *be* someone who refuses to just settle for whatever comes along."

"So that's that?"

"That's that," Autumn replied. This time, she simply outlined the heart in red and wrote in block letters, Happy Valentine's Day. She carefully placed it in Miranda's bouquet.

"That's that," she repeated tonelessly.

CHAPTER TEN

THE IRONY WAS, Autumn realized as Valentine's Day passed and February turned into March, then late March, that she was gradually, tentatively, reshaping her life exactly as Brad had wanted.

With only two months left on her lease, she'd begun to look for a different location for Sweet Sensations. When she moved to whatever site she decided on, it would only be the cookie bouquet part of the business she would take with her. And she could look forward to human hours—nine to five or six.

But it was because that was what *she* wanted, she reminded herself. It wasn't something she was doing to please anyone else.

Elaine had been wavering between driving to the new, "trendy" location to continue to work for Autumn or buying some of Autumn's excess equipment, staying here and keeping the bakery open on her own.

"I'll have to change the name if I stay, won't I?" Elaine said as they stood in the door they'd propped open so they could enjoy the bright afternoon that looked and felt like spring.

Autumn breathed in some of the warm fresh air. "You can keep it," she said with a generous grin. "We'll just make you a huge permanent Sweet Sensations display and you can call me when you get orders. I'll send people who need doughnuts to you."

"And then you'll charge me an outrageous fee and call me your first franchise," Elaine said dryly. "Yeah, sure."

"Yeah, sure," Autumn echoed. She was no longer certain if she wanted franchises or if Brad had been right about that, too. Had that whole scenario/idea been born because she was trying to impress her dad? She only knew that for now, she intended to play things by ear. Her own ear.

Inhaling deeply one more time, she went back to the kitchen. She still had the cookies for four bouquets to decorate before she could call it a day.

This would be the first month she'd actually end in the black. She'd realized that two days ago when she'd posted her day's totals. Business had steadily picked up since the dance—both the bakery and the bouquets so she couldn't credit it all to Brad, but she'd been fighting the urge to call him to say thanks. She wasn't sure she was strong enough to keep it simply that. And she wasn't sure it wasn't just a poor excuse to contact him.

He'd called her here a couple of times since then—strictly business—and Elaine had talked to him once and once to Betty. The rest of Autumn's official communication with him had been done by U.S. mail. There was no unfinished business with Barnett Marketing.

He'd left several messages at home in the week following the dance. Autumn hadn't returned those calls because she'd been sure they were personal. The number he'd left had been the one that only rang at his home.

"Autumn," Elaine said insistently and Autumn suspected that she'd said it several times. "I've locked up. Everything is done out front and ready for to-morrow. I guess I'll be on my way."

"Thanks, Elaine." The words held a lot more than appreciation for the few items Elaine had just described. Saying it felt good. She wanted to say it to Brad.

But instead of leaving, Elaine lingered. "I won't be able to do this if I keep the bakery going, will I?"

Autumn frowned as she lifted the cookie she'd just cut from the dough and molded it around the wooden "stem" in the pan. "To do what?"

"I won't be able to walk out of here at two o'clock and just forget about everything."

"No, you won't," Autumn agreed, "but like you said, with Nicki in school full time next year, you'll still probably be out of here in plenty of time to get home before the girls do."

"Without the cookie business, I won't have any reason to put in the extra hours you do."

"And you've made a lot of friends around here," Autumn said pointedly. "The customers really like you. I know you've been a big part of our success."

"Thanks." Elaine's dark eyes lit for a moment. "Hey, did I tell you what happened to Eric, the guy who ordered the valentine bouquet—the one who didn't want his girlfriend to think he was too serious . . ."

Autumn shook her head.

"He eloped last week," Elaine said with a laugh.

"Same girl?"

"Yep." Elaine smiled broadly. "Serves him right. And he's still a steady customer."

"Or he will be if you stay."

Elaine propped her hands on her hips and tilted her head suspiciously. "Sometimes, I get the impression you don't *want* me to go with you."

"I know I will never be lucky enough to find another employee—or friend—like you," Autumn told her, "but I think you'd be happy here. Elaine's Doughnuts? Elaine's Edibles? Sounds good, don't you think?" She sobered. "I want you to do whatever will make you happy."

"I want the same for you," Elaine said, then added impulsively. "Why don't you call him, Autumn?"

The suggestion came from nowhere but since Autumn hadn't been able to quit thinking about Brad all day, she didn't have to ask who "him" was. "I've been thinking about it," she admitted almost to herself.

"You have?"

Autumn held up a hand. "But it isn't like you think. Mostly I'd like to give him an update and thank him. He did make a big difference. Think how far we've come in the past six weeks."

"A long way," Elaine agreed, then hugged her from behind, careful not to mess up the cookie Autumn was shaping. She finally picked up her purse. "I'll see you in the morning. Call him," she commanded again as she closed the back door behind her.

"I think I will," Autumn muttered, stripping the gloves off her hands and taking a swig of cold coffee.

It took several minutes to get up the nerve. Her heart beat wildly as she dialed the phone. It seemed to drop to her toes as the answering service picked up. *Silly.* Since she had dialed his business number, of course the answering service would pick up the call, so the letdown was silly. And complete. She left her message.

She jumped as someone thumped on the front window. Sagging with relief when she saw who it was, she went to let them in.

"Dad. Shanna," she greeted them as she turned the latch.

"Is anything wrong," Shanna asked as she hurried in, concern wrinkling her normally placid face.

"No," Autumn answered slowly, frowning.

"The way you were leaning against the phone," Max explained, "we thought..."

"We were a bit worried," Shanna finished for him. "We thought you might have had bad news?"

Autumn managed a weary smile. "I'm just tired. And I just started one of those infamous games of telephone tag. You know how it is. But what are you two doing here in the middle of the day? Nothing's wrong, is it?"

The two of them exchanged a look that said exactly the opposite.

"Actually everything's right," Max said, grinning from ear to ear. "We have good news."

"That's why we were so concerned when we saw you," Shanna explained.

"We decided to take the afternoon off and we hoped you'd join us to celebrate," Max continued.

"What?" Autumn waited.

They exchanged another meaningful look. "We're getting married," her father said.

Though Autumn had expected the news for a long, long time, it still stunned her. She gaped at them.

Her father's face clouded in consternation and that brought her out of her daze. "It's about time," she cried and opened her arms to Shanna.

Max relaxed.

"So what finally brought this about?" she asked, turning to him to receive his bear hug.

Looking over his shoulder, Autumn saw Shanna's bemused look, as if she'd also like to hear the answer to that question, too.

"I guess I needed a nudge," Max said. "When you said something about it that evening we went out together, it suddenly dawned on me that, for all intents and purposes, you were grown, you have your own life. I realized I could get on with mine."

"Oh, Dad," Autumn said with more than a little exasperation. "You were waiting for me?"

"When you were younger, I thought there just wasn't time. Not without neglecting you. Successful relationships take time and attention. I guess I got in the habit of thinking that way."

"And in the meantime," Shanna added, "the relationship developed on its own."

The smile they shared made Autumn feel like a fifth wheel. "And, of course, none of the hesitation had anything to do with your first experience."

"That didn't make me anxious to rush into anything again," Max admitted.

"No one can accuse you of rushing," Shanna said dryly as Autumn opened her mouth to say pretty much the same thing and they all laughed.

"Guess this means I need to start looking for an apartment, too?"

"Too?" Max caught the verbal slip as Shanna protested.

"I have feelers out for a new, more visible location for the shop," Autumn said bluntly. "My lease expires here soon. I'm just going to be doing the cookie bouquets," she added. It seemed as good a time as any.

He took the news well. "Things really are going well?"

She nodded, and Shanna laced her hands through their arms. "That doesn't mean you have to move out."

"It's time, don't you think? I was going to do it anyway once I could pay my bills here."

"Sounds like we have a lot to celebrate." Max looked a little sad, contradicting the statement.

"So will you join us?" Shanna asked.

Autumn flung her arms around both of them again. "I'm so happy for you." She backed off. "But this looks like something just the two of you should celebrate. I've been an extra distraction too long already. Besides, I still have a couple of bouquets to do," she added when they looked as if they would argue. She herded them toward the door. She almost had them outside the door when the phone rang. "And don't expect me home this evening until very late," she thought to add with a wink. Her happiness for them spilled over in a giggle as Shanna—and her father, too—blushed furiously.

Then she hurried to the phone, grabbing it on the fourth ring. "Sweet Sensations," she said in a voice that shook. The butterflies in her stomach were an after effect of all the excitement, she reasoned.

For a second she thought it wasn't the call she'd been expecting, then she recognized Betty's businesslike tone.

"Autumn?"

Her heart plummeted to her toes.

"This is Betty, Barnett Marketing, returning your call. What can I do for you?"

He'd delegated the return call to Betty. That simple fact told Autumn more than she wanted to know. She had excused her call to him as a need to thank him, to give credit where credit was due. But when she'd dialed the phone, she'd still hoped...

She let it die.

"You...I..." She licked her dry lips and started over. "I just wanted to let Mr. Barnett know things are going very well," she managed to say calmly. "I wanted him to know his expertise worked wonders."

"I'm sure he'll be happy to hear that," Betty said.

"Will you pass on the message for me, Betty, along with my sincere thanks? He was right. He did magic. I'll always be grateful. I just wanted him to know," she said again.

"I will certainly tell him," Betty said cheerfully. "And you'll let us know if we can do anything else for you?"

"I'll let you know." Autumn assured her huskily. She cleared her throat. "Thanks, Betty," she added quickly and hung up.

The warm day had turned very cold. Autumn wrapped her arms around herself, hugging tightly. *I'm not going to cry. I'm not going to cry.*

The Easter egg and bunny bouquet she'd made for display that morning blurred before her eyes. She'd sold the two others—spring flowers like the ones she'd made for Brad's grandmother—and where there should be a deep sense of accomplishment and pride, there was an empty, hollow spot.

She'd blown it. She'd had her chance with Brad and had thrown it away. For pride.

She'd been trying to please her father all her life and her relationship with him was fine. Better than fine, she amended. And obviously, he'd been trying to please her, too. Hadn't he just admitted he'd waited so long to remarry because of her? What insanity had convinced her it was wrong to want to please someone else?

But at what price? She ached inside, knowing how lonely Max must have felt at times—for her sake. Shanna had been infatuated with the man for years. He'd wasted so much time.

He'd achieved everything he wanted . . . and had no one to share it with. Wouldn't the taste of success without someone to share it with be very bitter?

It was, she realized.

I'm not going to cry, she told herself again, then dashed a tear away, slowly sank to the floor behind the counter and sobbed like a baby. She'd never felt so alone.

"That was Brad," Elaine said a couple of days later, as she hung up the phone. He could have been just another customer who called or came in daily.

Autumn was cleaning the coffee machine. Their early-morning rush had just ended and after a short break, Elaine would watch the front and take care of customers while Autumn went to make a few more dozen doughnuts and started her bouquet orders for the day. Today, she only had two.

"Oh?" She took a deep breath, pressed a shaky hand against her chest and practiced her most casual smile. Betty must have given him her "thank you" message. She turned around slowly. Wiping the top of the display case, she worked her way toward Elaine.

"Guess what he wants?" Elaine waved a piece of paper in the air. "Another cookie bouquet." The edges of her grin turned down. "But only one this time."

"Oh?" Autumn said again and hoped she didn't sound like a broken record. *One. He'd narrowed his list to one. That meant—* "What kind of bouquet did he want?"

"Just the hearts and flowers thing again. Guess at least one of them must have been a success." She wriggled her eyebrows suggestively, then her expression fell. "Oh, Autumn, oh, hon. I'm sorry. I'm not thinking. You haven't said a word about him and I just assumed . . . well, it doesn't matter what I assumed. I obviously wasn't right."

Autumn pushed past her, into the kitchen. "When does he want it delivered?"

"He didn't say." Elaine followed her. "I mean, he doesn't want it delivered at all. Someone is picking it up this afternoon."

"Who?" Her heart pounded in her ears. She listened intently to hear Elaine's answer over the roar.

"He didn't say that, either, just that someone would be in before closing time unless I called his assistant back. I told him I didn't think having it done by then would be a problem."

"It won't." Autumn reached for a bowl and the dry ingredients she'd been keeping premixed since things had picked up. "I'll start it—and the others—now."

Elaine was watching her, licking her lips nervously, opening her mouth from time to time as if she wanted to say something. If she was waiting for Autumn to look at her directly, Autumn decided she'd wait forever. She wasn't about to look—or talk—about the searing pain in her head, or her heart. She'd obviously given too much away already.

And she for damn sure was going to be out of here when whoever—probably Brad—came to pick up the cookie bouquet.

Her friend seemed as relieved as she felt when the bell in the outer room clinked.

Only when the doors swung shut, separating her from Elaine's knowledgeable gaze, did Autumn let down her guard. She leaned wearily against the counter and closed her eyes.

This only verified that she'd missed her chance, she reminded herself. She'd known when he delegated the call to Betty that her feelings for him were hopeless. That it was too late.

This meant—she sucked in a huge breath and looked at the piece of paper Elaine had written the order on—he'd chosen someone. One. That was the key word.

No name. Miranda? Probably, Autumn admitted. After she'd distributed all his bouquets, Elaine had said that, given Brad's desire to marry someone who wasn't preoccupied with a career, Miranda was the most likely candidate. She lived with her mother in an elegant Plaza apartment. As far as Elaine could tell—she was in her housecoat at three in the afternoon, waving her hands around so her nails would dry—she didn't work. And from Autumn's own brief experience, she suspected Miranda's "thing" was playing social butterfly.

At least her goals and ambitions wouldn't interfere with Brad's dreams—unless she wasn't willing to have children.

A vision of Brad's son, with a mischievous face surrounded by dark hair and lit with brilliant blue eyes, brought another stab of pain. One thing was certain, since she'd never even been able to imagine herself married before Brad, she wouldn't marry anyone else. Without him, her life would be barren. No Brad, no children.

Elaine peeked back around the door and Autumn realized she'd been rolling this particular dough until it was paper thin. It was probably as tough as leather. She'd have to start over again.

"You okay?" Elaine asked softly.

Autumn nodded mutely as the bell rang again and for the next several hours, forced herself to concentrate only on her work.

By the time Elaine had donned her jacket to get Nicki from school, Autumn had planned her escape. "Elaine," she called her back from the door.

Elaine's wide eyes narrowed with concern as she turned back and Autumn redoubled her effort to keep her expression blank.

"Elaine, would you... could you stay? This afternoon, I mean? Go ahead and take Nicki out to lunch or something, take some time, then bring her back here? Would you mind staying today?" She swallowed hard. "Like you did before?"

Elaine hurried back to her and clasped her hand in a way that said more than any words. "Of course, hon. But are you sure? Maybe you and Brad need to see—"

"No." Autumn shook her head vehemently. "I want to be out of here by one-thirty, no later." She sighed and gave up her uncaring act. It wasn't fooling Elaine anyway. "It wouldn't do any good, Elaine. I'm absolutely, positively sure." She interrupted her friend's protest. "Look, you see right through me. What makes you think I wouldn't make a total fool of myself in front of him?"

Elaine didn't look happy with the situation, but nodded in agreement. "Nicki and I will be back in about an hour. Okay?" She stopped one more time by the door, as if remembering something important.

She gave Autumn a wide grin. "I may as well get used to longer hours anyway, since Jim and I had a long talk last night and I've decided to stay and run the bakery." She lifted her nose in the air. "You may consider me a fellow entrepreneur," she said airily, then raised her hand in a wave. "See you in a bit."

If Elaine's intent was to take Autumn's mind off Brad and give her something else to think about instead, it worked. Autumn actually found herself grinning once, until she noticed the clock was edging toward one.

She'd finished everything. The bouquets—one congratulation, one birthday and Brad's belated valentine—sat back in the kitchen, ready. Tomorrow morning's pastries were mixed. She looked out toward the parking lot for Elaine's metallic blue station wagon...and about had a heart attack.

Brad was there, getting out of his car.

The spring wind ruffled his dark hair, lacing through it and leaving fascinating little waves behind. He gazed around him, seemingly without a care in the world, then squinted into the bright sun, toward her shop.

She backed away, further into the shadows and drank in the sight of him.

She'd never seen his arms, she realized as she admired the way his polo shirt hugged his chest and emphasized the fresh tan on his arms. He'd always worn loose sweaters—and one time a tuxedo. She caught her breath as he leaned back in to get something out of his car, displaying himself from an interesting angle. She'd never noticed the cute little way his butt curved, either.

He took a step toward the shop and reality sunk in. Autumn panicked. Her mind frantically considered her options: locking the door, hiding in the kitchen . . . anything. She heard the solid thud of the back door closing.

"Autumn? Sorry. It took a little longer than I intended. We had to run by home," Elaine said as Autumn burst into the kitchen. "Nicki fingerpainted at school tod— Hey! What's wrong?"

"Thank God, you're here," Autumn managed to get out. "Brad—"

The bell over the outer door clanged and Autumn shivered.

"I'll take care of it," Elaine mouthed calmly. "Nicki, I'll be back in a minute, then we'll get you settled with some crayons or something. Okay?"

Elaine set down her purse and the bag of things she'd brought for Nicki to do, then she pushed through the door. "Oh, hi, Brad," Autumn heard her say. She covered her mouth with her fingers and tried to quit shaking.

"Did you make any special cookies, today?" Nicki asked in her sweet high voice. Taking off her small jacket, she looked helplessly from Autumn to the high hook where it belonged.

It took a second for Autumn's mind to begin working again. "Here," she found herself whispering. "Let me get it for you." The further she got from the other room, the easier breathing became.

"Why are you whispering?" Nicki said in what sounded to Autumn like a yell.

"I . . . I don't know," she managed to answer in a soft, but almost normal tone. "I guess it just seemed like the right thing to do." She hung the coat up and reached down for Nicki's hand. "I did make a very special cookie, just for you," she said. "Wanna see?" With the extra dough she'd had that morning,

Autumn had woven a small basket, complete with a tiny flower in it. She placed it carefully in her companion's small hand.

The door from the other room burst open and Autumn froze. Elaine stepped in and picked up Brad's bouquet. Her glance at Autumn was reassuring. As she started to leave again, Nicki skipped after her.

Autumn saw a disaster in the making and rushed after both of them. Either the door was going to swing back and hit Nicki, or—if Elaine saw her daughter in time and tried to catch it—the bouquet was certain to get the crushing impact.

Autumn caught and held the door open as Nicki rushed through on Elaine's heels.

"Look, Mama. See what Autumn gave me." The little girl's excited voice seemed to fill both rooms.

Everything seemed to stop, even time.

"Autumn's here?" Brad asked in a low voice.

She heard a sharp intake of air and glanced up, directly into his eyes.

CHAPTER ELEVEN

FOR A SECOND, Autumn thought she saw pain there, then his slow, easy grin spread from his lips to gradually fill his wonderful eyes.

"I thought I'd missed you," he said casually, shifting something in his arms.

"I was ... just on my way out." She let go of the door.

She'd barely made it to the coatrack to get her purse and jacket when she heard the door behind her open again.

"Wouldn't you like to see what I brought you?"

Autumn spun around. Elaine was peeking around him, grimacing as she shrugged helplessly. The door swung shut again, leaving them alone.

"Listen. I'm really late. I have ... somewhere I ... have to be ..." She waved to some vague spot behind her.

"Running away again?" he asked softly.

She gave up. She knew she was going to cry in a minute. He looked so good. She was helplessly, hopelessly in love with him. She closed her eyes. Every ounce of the energy she'd reserved for her escape left her and she felt her whole body sag weakly. "Oh, Brad," she whispered.

"Oh, Autumn," he said, but this time he was only inches away. She felt his warm, sweet breath on her face and opened her eyes again. He filled her vision.

"What do we have left to say?" she asked. "You're going to get married, aren't you?"

"Maybe," he admitted. "In the past few weeks, I've discovered I'm a whole lot pickier than I thought I was."

Pickier? Pickier than he was? What now? Had he decided his wife would have to be joined with him at the hip and never leave his side?

That thought almost did her in. After six weeks of not seeing him, the thought of never leaving his side didn't sound like the life sentence it should. It sounded incredibly appealing. And being joined at the hip? Sharing intimacies with him? Being possessed by Mr. Brad Barnett, macho man extraordinaire? It had to be the next best thing to heaven.

"Pickier?" she asked.

"Yeah," he said softly. "I thought just about any woman who filled certain requirements would do. I thought I could just pick one, marry her and live happily ever after. I've found there's one in particular I want. I don't think any other will do. If that's not picky, I don't know what is."

She didn't dare hope. She forced herself to back a step away. "And is that who the bouquet's for?" Glancing down, she realized the bouquet he held cradled in one arm wasn't the one she'd made. Her eyes widened. It wasn't one anyone with any sense had made.

"Where did you get that?"

He laughed, still close enough to make her feel the vibrations from the low, sexy rumble. "That's what I brought you. I don't think you have to worry about the competition, do you?"

She squinted, trying to get a better look. He moved back and placed it on her worktable, under the fluorescent lights.

"That's bad." She giggled. "That's really bad."

The cookies were chocolate chip. They weren't frosted or decorated in any way. Instead of the bright colored tissue paper, which acted as filler exactly as greenery did in a regular flower bouquet, this one had crumpled newspaper. But what was really odd was the shapes of the cookies themselves. They were indistinct, unrecognizable.

"What are they? Where'd you get it?" she repeated. She looked up at him again and suddenly didn't care.

He was grinning from ear to ear. He pulled one of the cookies from the bouquet. "You can't tell what this is?" he asked mock-indig...antly.

The cookie was a long, narrow, angled, rectangular shape, wide and square at the top and pointy at the bottom. "Am I supposed to be able to?"

"It's Florida." He pulled another squarish one. "And this is Montana."

She gazed at Florida and narrowed her eyes. If she tried real hard and pictured a whole United States map, she could maybe see it. "Oh."

"Hawaii's at the bottom of the basket," he said. "It's really difficult to put all those little pieces on a stick."

She laughed. She wanted desperately to fall into his arms. God help her. She loved him. And the way he was looking at her surely had to mean something.

"So do you want to tell me the significance of all this?" she asked, looking at the bouquet again, forcing herself to concentrate on something besides him, trying to tell if she could recognize any of the states without his help.

"These are the states you should try to put franchises in first."

She frowned. Was this his peace offering? Was he saying he wanted to be friends, business contacts, even if there could be nothing else? That was the relationship he said he maintained with some of the names on his original list. "Florida?"

"Great golf," he said.

"Montana?"

"I have a friend with a spread there. See how I picked up the lingo? I just spent three weeks there. Getting out on a ranch and playing cowboy is a kick for us city boys."

Golf? Us city boys? He was going to help her market her franchises now? She knew her frown had turned into an incomprehensible scowl now. And she couldn't help it. She could smell his subtle cologne. The warmth of his fingers on her arm seemed to be spreading a warmth all over. She latched on to the one thing he'd said that she understood. "You've been out of town? In Montana?"

"Yes."

"Among other places. I stopped in Chicago first and saw Vanessa."

"How is Vanessa?"

Somehow, during the last few statements, he'd moved closer again. He was only inches away. "Do we really have to talk about her right now? She's back with her husband," he added quickly, as if the best thing would be getting it over with. "They're working things out."

His breath fanned her face. His arm crept around her and drew her into his embrace.

"Good," Autumn managed to say. "I'm glad."

"I could only stay with Vanessa two days," he said, his gaze on her mouth. "They're so much in love, it hurts to watch. And then I'd call Betty to see if you had called and you hadn't." His words got softer and softer and came more quickly, like a flood. "And I'd see them, slowly, happily working out their differences and it just reminded me of my differences with you." He groaned. "Dammit, Autumn, can I kiss you now?" His voice turned husky. "Have I said anything that makes you believe we can work something out ourselves? Somehow?"

He didn't wait for a reply. His lips covered hers, lightly for a second, then with a hunger she thought might consume her.

She hoped it would. Nothing in her world had ever tasted so sweet. Nothing in her fantasies had ever held such bliss.

Her hand curled against his roughly textured cheek. He was real. He was here. And he wanted her, cookie bouquets and franchises and all.

She wrapped her arms around his neck and clung. He kissed her, hugged her close, left ticklish nibbles down the side of her neck, whispered sweet words in her ears, then hugged her and kissed her again.

She kissed him back until she hoped his knees were as weak as hers and his head was spinning.

She didn't know if they ever would have stopped if Elaine hadn't come in and cleared her throat loudly. When they both looked over at her, she said primly, "There are children here, you know." She ruined it by laughing.

Autumn buried her hot face in Brad's solid chest.

"Come on, you two, get out of here," Elaine continued, coming into the kitchen with them, making shooing motions. "Next thing I know, I'll have throw cold water on you or drag you off the worktable or something."

Brad looked at the stainless-steel equipment, shook his head and grabbed Autumn's hand. "She may be right. It's time to get out of here."

She barely had enough time to grab her purse before he towed her toward the front door.

Nicki's eyes lit up when she saw him. "Mr. Brad, don't you want to color with me?"

"I don't think so right now," Elaine answered for him with a suppressed laugh. "I'll see you in the morning, Autumn," she called.

"Maybe," Brad said, never taking his gaze from Autumn. At least not until they got to his car and she hesitated. "Shouldn't I get my car? The bouquets. We forgot the bouquets."

"Get in," he growled, hitting the automatic lock buttons on the side of his door. "We have time to worry about all that later."

Autumn did as she was told.

Brad jammed his keys into the ignition and paused only long enough to lean across and kiss her again before he put it into motion.

"Where are we going?"

"Home!"

"Your home?"

"Our home." He took his eyes off the road for a second. "At least if you'll decide to have me."

Autumn felt joy surge through her veins. She thought her heart would burst with the overwhelming abundance of happiness and love. But he hadn't said it. He hadn't actually said love—yet.

"I guess it depends on why you want me," she said.

He looked at her warningly. "You haven't figured it out yet?"

"Besides sex," she said. "I mean besides sex."

"I think it's called making love if it's done the way I intend us to do it," he said roughly.

"Oh? And how's that?"

For a second, his expression said he was going to jam the brakes, stop right in the middle of the highway and show her. Then he turned serious. "It's a good thing we have this drive ahead of us," he said. "I have the feeling it's the only way I could possibly say all the things I need to say to you without getting sidetracked."

Her heart flip-flopped inside her chest as he laced the fingers of his free hand through hers.

"And what is it you want to tell me," she asked seriously.

"That I love you." He punctuated it by raising her hand and kissing her fingertips. "That I need you." He did it again, only this time, the kiss landed on the back of her hand. "That I want to marry you and I don't care anymore what you plan to do with your time and energy, as long as you save some of both for me." That one was on her wrist.

"And our children?"

"And our children," he confirmed. Higher still.

His punctuation marks were by far the most intriguing she'd ever discovered. At this rate, it would be interesting to see where his kisses were landing by the time they got to his house. "I've been doing a lot of thinking about my time and energy, too," she said to distract herself from that thought.

Then she told him about her search for a new location, about Elaine's plan to takeover the bakery, Max and Shanna's plans for a wedding, about the aching need she'd felt to share with him all the developments in her life the past six weeks. She'd known him such a short time. How could she have missed him so?

"I missed you," she said in a whisper.

He slowed to take his exit. His gaze locked on hers for a moment. "I've missed you."

She cleared her throat. "You should know—" she lightened her tone "—I'm not sure I'm interested in franchises anymore. I hope you won't be too disappointed if the Florida thing doesn't work out." She giggled. "Whatever made you think of a Florida cookie, anyway?"

He sighed. "I guess on the plane to Montana, I was thinking about how much I love anticipating going places, wondering if I could give that up for you, the way I'd expected you to give up your dreams for me. It suddenly occurred to me that if you did start franchising, you'd probably have to do a *lot* of traveling at first and it wouldn't be too bad if we could do it together."

"And go the places you want to go, of course."

He smiled. "That's negotiable."

"And while we're there, you'll play golf and do a little marketing for me?"

"That's the plan," he said with a chuckle. "You'll be happy to know I've decided to give you a good deal on my fees."

"Thanks," she said dryly as he turned the corner down his street. "But don't expect me to give you a good deal on bouquets for all your old girlfriends," she warned.

He laughed and punched a button over his visor. His garage door began its steady climb upward as he swung the car into the driveway.

"Which reminds me. Who was the bouquet you ordered today for?"

"Me. I had to have an excuse to come see you, didn't I?"

"You could have just come."

"I'm sure that would have been my next move. You obviously weren't going to come to me."

"I thought it was hopeless," she breathed as he leaned over to kiss her. "When you didn't even return my call..."

"I came home from Montana as soon as Betty gave me your message. I couldn't have stayed away much longer anyway."

She sighed contentedly as he turned off the car and closed the garage door behind them.

"That had to be record time for that trip."

"Record time," he agreed. "I've never been more anxious to get somewhere."

The dimness of the car and the dark garage feigned nightfall. Autumn touched him to verify, once again, that it was not a dream.

He kissed her palm. "If you have anything else you want to say or ask me, you'd better ask now," he warned. "When I get you in that house, I have no intention of wasting my breath on conversation. Not for a long, long time."

"You'll have to take me to work in the morning," she said pointedly.

"Okay, not for at least twelve hours or so. Anything else?" He stole another kiss.

She giggled. "Who made that horrible bouquet?"

He snorted indignantly. "You'll see in a minute. My kitchen's a mess. Refrigerator cookie dough and crumbs and parts and pieces everywhere."

"You? What'd you use for cookie cutters?"

"Puzzle pieces. I had to enlarge them but I have a U.S. map puzzle from—"

Her giggle turned into full blown laughter. He hushed her the only way he knew how, only to stop a minute later and suggest seductively that they get out of the car. He opened his door, casting light across them.

She hadn't budged.

"Why do I get the impressions you're reluctant to get out of this car?" he asked, searching her face.

"Maybe because I am."

"Why?" he asked gently, stroking her hair back and hooking it behind her ear.

"Because I've never—" She stopped short and felt her face warm at what she was about to admit to him. But somehow, it seemed important.

He waited patiently.

Gazing down at the fingers she'd laced together in her lap, she chose her words carefully. "I've never been able to commit myself to the...kind of relationship you're talking about." She risked a peek up at him.

He looked stunned, then pleased. The corner of his mouth quirked. "I'm delighted to know you've never been married."

"That's—that wasn't what I was talking about."

"Oh," he said knowingly. "You'll be delighted to know, I'm not interested in any kind of relationship with you besides the long-term, lifetime kind. I want it all legal, signed, sealed and delivered in writing as soon as possible. And I would hope that includes...whatever you *are* talking about."

She bit her lip shyly. "Of course. I just thought...I should warn you."

"Forewarned," he said softly, "is forearmed." Then he drew her into his arms and kissed her with a passion she'd only glimpsed until now. By the time he drew away this time, she was shaking with need and frustration. She groaned, but didn't open her eyes.

"I want you," he said. "I need you. But mostly, I love you. I don't want anything from you that you aren't willing and anxious to give. Not until you're ready. Say the word, I'll take you home."

"I thought you said we were home," she sighed, holding out her arms. "Please, take me the rest of the way."

He complied.

FREE VALENTINE'S BROOCH! $9.95 U.S. retail value

This Valentine's Day Harlequin brings you all the essentials—romance, chocolate and jewelry—in:

VALENTINE *Delights*

Matchmaking chocolate-shop owner Papa Valentine dispenses sinful desserts, mouth-watering chocolates...and advice to the lovelorn, in this collection of three delightfully romantic stories by Meryl Sawyer, Kate Hoffmann and Gina Wilkins.

As our special Valentine's Day gift to you, each copy of *Valentine Delights* will have a beautiful, filigreed, heart-shaped brooch attached to the cover.

Make this your most delicious Valentine's Day ever with *Valentine Delights!*

Available in February wherever Harlequin books are sold.

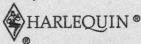

HARLEQUIN ®

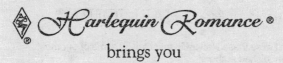

Harlequin Romance ®

brings you

PENNINGTON

a place where dreams come true...

Welcome to Pennington, the fictional town in the heart of England created by popular author Catherine George.

Surrounded by lush countryside, with quaint tearooms and public gardens ablaze with flowers, Pennington is full of charm—the perfect place to find romance!

This delightful English town is the setting for future romances by Catherine George.

Next month watch for:

#3449 THE SECOND BRIDE

Rufus Grierson had married Jo's best friend—but when his wife was taken from him so tragically, Rufus found himself turning to Jo for comfort. Shared grief led to passion...and to pregnancy. Rufus insisted on marriage, but was he only interested in his unborn child—not the love Jo longed to share with him?

Available in March wherever
Harlequin books are sold.

HARLEQUIN®

Don't miss these Harlequin favorites by some of our most distinguished authors!
And now, you can receive a discount by ordering two or more titles!

HT#25645	THREE GROOMS AND A WIFE by JoAnn Ross	$3.25 U.S.	$3.75 CAN.	☐
HT#25647	NOT THIS GUY by Glenda Sanders	$3.25 U.S.	$3.75 CAN.	☐
HP#11725	THE WRONG KIND OF WIFE by Roberta Leigh	$3.25 U.S.	$3.75 CAN.	☐
HP#11755	TIGER EYES by Robyn Donald	$3.25 U.S.	$3.75 CAN.	☐
HR#03416	A WIFE IN WAITING by Jessica Steele	$3.25 U.S.	$3.75 CAN.	☐
HR#03419	KIT AND THE COWBOY by Rebecca Winters	$3.25 U.S.	$3.75 CAN.	☐
HS#70622	KIM & THE COWBOY by Margot Dalton	$3.50 U.S.	$3.99 CAN.	☐
HS#70642	MONDAY'S CHILD by Janice Kaiser	$3.75 U.S.	$4.25 CAN.	☐
HI#22342	BABY VS. THE BAR by M.J. Rodgers	$3.50 U.S.	$3.99 CAN.	☐
HI#22382	SEE ME IN YOUR DREAMS by Patricia Rosemoor	$3.75 U.S.	$4.25 CAN.	☐
HAR#16538	KISSED BY THE SEA by Rebecca Flanders	$3.50 U.S.	$3.99 CAN.	☐
HAR#16603	MOMMY ON BOARD by Muriel Jensen	$3.50 U.S.	$3.99 CAN.	☐
HH#28885	DESERT ROGUE by Erine Yorke	$4.50 U.S.	$4.99 CAN.	☐
HH#28911	THE NORMAN'S HEART by Margaret Moore	$4.50 U.S.	$4.99 CAN.	☐

(limited quantities available on certain titles)

	AMOUNT	$
DEDUCT:	**10% DISCOUNT FOR 2+ BOOKS**	$
ADD:	**POSTAGE & HANDLING**	$
	($1.00 for one book, 50¢ for each additional)	
	APPLICABLE TAXES*	$_____
	TOTAL PAYABLE	$_____
	(check or money order—please do not send cash)	

To order, complete this form and send it, along with a check or money order for the total above, payable to Harlequin Books, to: **In the U.S.:** 3010 Walden Avenue, P.O. Box 9047, Buffalo, NY 14269-9047; **In Canada:** P.O. Box 613, Fort Erie, Ontario, L2A 5X3.

Name: _____

Address: _____ City: _____

State/Prov.: _____ Zip/Postal Code: _____

*New York residents remit applicable sales taxes.
  Canadian residents remit applicable GST and provincial taxes.
Look us up on-line at: http://www.romance.net

HBACK-JM4